## About the author

Michael Short, originally from New York, lives in San Diego, is married, and has two children. He attended the University of California, San Diego, receiving a degree in sociology and a minor in history. He has worked extensively with the homeless and poor and is an advocate for addressing the issues facing society today. His writing touches on the themes of destiny, redemption, and the power of love to transform people's lives. His interests include book collecting and reading classical literature. This is his first novel. He is currently working on a prequel to Cool Girl.

COOL GIRL

# Michael Short

## COOL GIRL

Vanguard Press

VANGUARD PAPERBACK

© Copyright 2024
**Michael Short**

The right of Michael Short to be identified as author of
this work has been asserted by him in accordance with the
Copyright, Designs and Patents Act 1988.

**All Rights Reserved**

No reproduction, copy or transmission of this publication
may be made without written permission.
No paragraph of this publication may be reproduced,
copied or transmitted save with the written permission of the publisher, or
in accordance with the provisions
of the Copyright Act 1956 (as amended).

Any person who commits any unauthorised act in relation to this
publication may be liable to criminal prosecution and civil claims for
damages.

A CIP catalogue record for this title is available from the British Library.

ISBN 978-1-83794-222-0

This is a work of fiction. Names, characters, businesses, places, events
and incidents are either the products of the author's imagination or are
used in a fictitious manner. Any resemblance to actual persons, living or
dead, or actual events is purely coincidental.

*Vanguard Press is an imprint of*
*Pegasus Elliot Mackenzie Publishers Ltd.*
www.pegasuspublishers.com

First Published in 2024

**Vanguard Press**
**Sheraton House  Castle Park**
**Cambridge  England**

Printed & Bound in Great Britain

To my wife, Marilyn, who was the inspiration for this book, whose love is kind, patient, and never fails, this work is affectionately dedicated

# CHAPTER ONE

"You said you loved me," she whispered close to his ear. "Remember?"

John, with his arm hooked in hers, looked directly at her, puzzled, stern, and replied, "I did?"

"Yes, silly," Ernestine continued. "You remember; don't fake it like you didn't say it… you said it at the height of our lovemaking yesterday."

"If I did, I must have meant it," was the quick, ineffectual reply, a joking tone in the assertion.

They were both at the beach, the Pacific Ocean roaring a few yards away, on a boardwalk bench, watching the waves roll in, on a cloudy June day in 1982.

"You do care for me, don't you?" she said, pestering him in his silence, with her hair flowing in the wind.

He took off his sunglasses, inhaled deeply, looked at this beautiful, elegant girl he had been dating for the last three years, and calmly said, "Yes, you know I do. Why keep asking? I get it, you want to trap me, get a reaction out of me, right?"

"No, not at all. A girl needs to know where she stands. She wants a commitment and marriage."

They both stared at the ocean; it was peaceful, the day bright, a few surfers in the currents, and several people walking along the edge of the water. They were inspired by it all, carefree, easy, no one to bother them.

Surprisingly, he said, his voice wavering, his face pale, "Yes, let's set a date. We need to plan things through." He went on and on in his practicality of planning and expenses. She listened initially because she got her… yes, her love, her commitment. John stood up, then knelt on one knee as Ernestine sat numb on the bench. "Ernestine, will you marry me?"

She knew it was hard to say from this shy, quiet man. She whispered, "Yes, of course."

They continued to sit at that bench, now entrenched in their memory forever, for several minutes, their hands touching each other. Ernestine began to whimper in her happiness, and John sat, nervous, not fully realizing what he had just said. These two youths were euphoric; they slouched on that bench as they gazed at the bright horizon. But all of this was to take a tragic detour in their young lives. John was to receive a phone call from a woman in his recent past that threatened to change everything.

If you know John and Ernestine's story and history, you will know that they met three years ago, at a Downtown San Diego theatre, and then went to a hotel nearby and had an illicit rendezvous. It was bold, exciting, and a bit forbidden. Since then, John graduated from college with his degree, located a job, and found a shared apartment in La Mesa. Once a young, immature college student, now John Earley is a brash, self-assured young man at twenty-three. He is white, six foot two, with curly brown hair, a distinctive flowing red-brown mustache, translucent green eyes, and a trim, athletic body. He is soft spoken, friendly, and easy to get along with. He is Catholic and his passion is book reading.

They have forged a true relationship over time, with all its foibles, stares, and avoidances from people that see them only as a mixed-race couple; they wonder who they are, why they are attracted to each other, what is the hidden message for their love? Ernestine Jones, Black, now twenty-seven, a nurse, is strikingly beautiful. She stands a proud five nine, with a trim figure, fully developed breasts, a narrow chin, pronounced cheekbones that a model would desire, and large, captivating brown eyes. People who meet her say she is ebullient, vivacious, and someone you want to know. She decided to move out of her mother's house three years ago and live by herself, with no guilt, not looking back at her boyfriend at the time, Spencer. She located an old, quaint one-bedroom apartment overlooking a garage in a sleepy middle-class neighborhood. Ernestine, in sum, is a classy girl who likes fashion, designer clothes, and listens religiously to soft jazz music.

After leaving the beach arm in arm, snuggled together with Ernestine so happy and giggling, the two jumped into John's blue Pontiac T1000, a small car with a hatchback. He started the engine and went down the road, headed to the highway going east. Ernestine prodded, "Are you going to tell your mother right away about the news?"

He paused, grimaced, and answered, "Of course, eventually. Let me get used to the feeling. In a few days, I don't know."

She felt his hesitation with his domineering, quiet mother. "How is your mother?" she pursued.

"Same as always. She is taking care of the Prodigal Son, my brother who can't seem to stay out of trouble and focused. Those two should be married to each other. I don't get my mom's control over everybody and everything."

"Yeah, I know how she can be. It took her about a year to warm up to me. In fact, I did not meet your mom until we had been dating about six months." She was facing toward him in the bucket-seated car with her legs crossed, and she stroked the side of his face.

"I wish I could have changed that, but my mom is a little neurotic and controlling. She doesn't trust everyone at first and comes off like a cold fish. She's too guarded and frumpy. I don't care anyway; we are moving on with our lives whether people like us or not, its's their loss." His tone was forceful and palliative as he gripped the steering wheel tightly. He looked at his girl, in all her splendor, radiant, still smiling, and demure. He found her, at this moment, very desirable, and wished to kiss her. A tear began to form in his eye, which he quickly wiped away so she would not see it.

He continued his tirade, "My mom! I can't believe I ever got out of that dungeon, but I had to. I couldn't take it any longer; it was so oppressive at times and would just leave the whole day not to face those two and come back in time for dinner and then sleep. If it wasn't for my drive to get an education and degree, I would be dead by now. I had to find a job, any job."

"You got one, a good one. It is in the field you always wanted to be in. I think that is impressive." She began playing with her curls, pawing his face, and wished she could take him to bed right now. She studied him, so calm, so matter of fact, so assured, now much different from when he was twenty – three years ago: life changed, people find new experiences and meet individuals who pull you into a new direction, gaining confidence, making mistakes, and learning along the way. This is what young Earley experienced in the last three years in living and knowing Ernestine.

"It takes time," he asserted, looking at her instead of the road. "All good things take their time. Look at us: we had to overcome a ton of crap, that ass of a boyfriend, drunk, trying to visit your mom all the time, and that Brenda – boy, she is a charm, chain-smoking and her rude ways. Your mom, though, she was supportive but quiet about our dating. I could not figure her out."

"Me neither," she commented. "You don't have any regrets?"

"None, never. I don't live in regrets."

"Do you wish you were dating someone else… of your own race?"

He paused and reflected. "That's dumb. You ask me that after three years? You are the most beautiful woman I have ever seen. Don't forget that."

She was comforted by the thought, and she got closer to him, distracting his driving, her perfume potent. He stared at her sultry eyes, with the dark eyelashes, trimmed eyebrows, perfect makeup: she could have been a model like Beverly Johnson, he thought. Yes, but I don't want to lose her to an endless career on the road, with distractions, and surly groping men all around. No, that won't do.

"Are you nervous, honey?" he inquired.

"About the engagement, marriage…? No, not really. I am just a little anxious that you may change your mind or have second thoughts."

"Like I said, never; there is no one else. I haven't dated anyone since we met. Trust, that is important; in fact, it is the most important thing to move forward."

"You're right, and I know it. I want it to be special and plan out our finances, and who to invite and not to invite." She emphasized the last few words to exclude recalcitrant family members who didn't approve of the arrangement.

"I'm not sure of things, too, like should I have my brother at the wedding? He just got back from the navy, who kicked his ass out on a dishonorable discharge. He can be rude at times and has personal issues."

"Why did they kick him out?" she asked.

"You got me," he answered, annoyed. "Must have been his attitude and not following orders. Or he had some type of mental breakdown."

"I see," she calmly said. "I have a couple of real winners in my family, too. My sister, she's a real work of art. She goes out at all hours of the night with these worthless homeboys. She better be careful, or she will wind up pregnant and in a mess, with no guy to take care of her. Those type of men just screw girls and leave them once the baby is born. Brenda did get a job, finally, at a retail store, but she just lives for the moment, spending all her money on pot, beer, and loose men who are going nowhere. It's sad."

She stopped talking as the car neared his apartment, east toward La Mesa, a quiet upscale neighborhood filled with ritzy homes, and no one seen outside running the streets, with a large cluster of apartments and condominiums, spacious, clean, with carports. The town was filled with stores, outlets, thrift stores, antiques shops, but in the summer it was oppressively warm.

"I wonder if my dad will come to the wedding," Ernestine said fretfully. "He lives way out in Arizona. I haven't talked to him in a while. I bet he is wrapped up in that stupid younger woman that lives with him." She did not mention her name, on purpose, and her tone was of disapproval.

"Honey, I would not worry about it. If they show, they show. It's your dad, he will be glad to show up; after all, it's going to be a big event, the talk of the town!" John was becoming excited, and he searched her face. He added, "I know you love him. He'll be there, promise." His mannerism was deferential, caring, reaching out to help; it was the soul of his profession as a social worker to solve the ills and troubles of people.

Ernestine was quiet, reserved, unsure of herself and her feelings; she tried to solve the dilemma of the lost dad, with his floozy in Arizona, but she never visited the place or was invited, as if Jerry Jones had a dirty secret or life to hide. He was well off, living on his army pension and working part-time, and he had been gone out of her life for over fifteen years. He was distant, but he would call every so often to talk with family in idle, safe words like "How's the family? Do you have a job? Do you need anything?" Stupid, trite phrases that did not mean much to her. Now, at the critical point of the engagement, he will be summoned to come home and face mother and sister, and meet her fiancé, who was white. How does she explain that? Should she explain it? What if there is an argument over the past life, the separation, the cheating, the hiding out? It was too much for her to consider now.

"What do you want to do today?" John added, breaking Ernestine's reverie.

"Oh, I don't know. Maybe have some lunch and a romp in the hay." She said this coyly out of nowhere, a finger to her lip. "Will your roommate be home?"

"I hope not. He can be the most annoying guy around. Always cleaning the apartment. I never see him out on a date. He did mention, though, a switch, of meeting some Vietnamese girl who said to his face, 'You going to like it', with that accent. You know what she was referring to." He delighted in the telling of this, but was derisive toward his roommate, who seemed to not commit to anyone or anything that he said or stood for. Ron Miller was indeed a mysterious bird, unfathomable. He never said what he truly meant; he would tell you only what he wanted to in bits and pieces. John, in sum, thought he was a conflicted man.

The car pulled into the assigned space. John got out quickly and opened the passenger door for Ernestine, who elegantly got out, slowly, with her designer Louis Vuitton purse in the crook of her arm. He noticed, vividly, her perfect, slender hands with immaculate, red nail polish, no chips, and her arms were toned in the short-sleeve shirt. He continued to study her as she walked and wiggled in her high heels up the ramp to the large, two-bedroom apartment on the corner of the building. They entered, tentatively, the dark, stale unit, the blinds drawn: no one was at home. It was peaceful now, and no one was to be seen around the complex, like a cemetery. Ernestine entered first, the dressy heels making a scraping noise at the metal door entrance, as John softly patted her firm behind.

In the middle of the living room, with its brown shag carpet, she turned around, dropped the purse on the sofa, took off her hoop earrings and demanded, "Come on, sweetheart, let's go to the room." She wore a serious, determined demeanor, and she looked him up and down lustfully. He pulled her by the hand to his bedroom, closed and locked the door quietly, and frantically began removing his clothes.

She was breathing on the back of his neck from behind, eager, with her hands rubbing the side of his thighs. Her chin was on his muscular shoulder. Ernestine was naked, aggressive, pawing his chest, and she led him to the bed. She whispered, "Let's make this special. I want you to love me for a long time."

Her words aroused him further, and he began kissing her thin, smooth neck and inhaled her perfume. He then began to search all her body, reveling in it and its perfection, as he began caressing her ample breasts. They were lost in a frenzy, and she grabbed his extension as he lay flat on the bed, legs apart, her total slave. She continued to fondle and encourage his rising erection. "That feels great," he said.

Ernestine, looking up at him, answered with a half laugh, "You have not seen nothing yet." Her lips became puckered, and she acted like she was on a dirty secret mission to give him all the pleasure she had, all her love, all her life, there, in that double bed, today, this day of commitment. She was on top of him quickly now, her eyes half closed, the curtains drawn, making the room dark, and not a sound was to be heard except their moaning and erratic breathing. He grabbed her soft, generous hips as she continued her teasing motions, moving, circulating, her hands reaching out to his hairy chest. She took her time with him, and, in a flash, she recalled the first excitement of that hotel room three years prior and the thrill of it all to be different, with someone outside of her race to share her love with. Today, they were in unison, they were in ecstasy, they enjoyed every part of their bodies, the crevices, the minutes that passed by in their coupling that was so natural and uninhibited.

When it was over, they lay side by side, depleted, on the messy sheets, with two glasses of wine John had got from the kitchen. They were still stroking each other's arms and bodies. John, in a flash of emotion, said, "That was great, girl."

"You weren't so bad yourself, lover boy," she responded affirmatively with a grunt. She searched his face, and saw he was really relaxed, joyful, not a care in the world presently. She sipped her wine with an approving look on her face, her eyebrows raised. She then inquired, "What is the plan for the day? It's still early, around noon. Want to have lunch, my treat?"

"Let's grab some sandwiches at the deli across the street" – his hands extended, showing the enormous size of them – "and a cold brew. After that, maybe a movie… What's playing?"

"That tearjerker everyone is talking about: *Grease 2*," she idly said. Some stupid movie with all white people in it, she thought, never any people of color, any color, all the same, all bland. She did admit that there were some good movies played by the usual actors, but it would be nice to see a Sidney Poitier or Sammy Davis Jr type in these flicks. She also had to tread lightly on John's feelings and life; he could not change the way the establishment is, or was. She knew, deep down, that he was a rebel, a crusader for the Black folks, and all ethnicities, in their struggle to be recognized in the cinema and other areas of society.

"*Grease 2* sounds boring. Is that the one with Michelle Pfeiffer?" he asked, squinting in derision.

"Not sure who is in it. We can go and check it out, or see some good horror flick. That would be more entertaining."

John stroked her soft hair on the bed and put his hand under her chin and said, "Whatever we decide to do, I will be your king for a day."

Puzzled, frowning, she inquired, "King for a day, what's that?"

"Don't you remember, when we first me at the theater, before we went to our little secret rendezvous, you said, 'I'll be your queen for a day'? I never forgot that line, so assured, so great. You still are my queen."

She laughed quietly, then got up. "I said that! I must have been drunk or real stupid. Funny you thought about it after all this time. Queen, queen, sounds good… I guess I am a Queen Elizabeth. At least, today, I feel so." She said this so calmly, as if it was really true, real, already ingrained in her spirit, always there, regal, the way she so fervently carried herself in the real world, trying to prove her worth as a black woman, always needing to excel, be a little better than the competition, whether at work, in the mall, at the store, anywhere she needed to get goods and services, without fear of ostracism, ignorance, or avoidance by the power elite.

"I'll get dressed and we'll head out," she added, trying to keep her mood pleasant for him.

Suddenly, the door flew open to the apartment and Ron, the roommate, was there with two heavy bags at his side. "Hello, hello! Anyone home!" he said as loud as he could in case anyone was doing something private. He saw John come out of the bedroom, and added, "Hey, partner, what's the haps?" He used this slang word 'haps' to fit into the cool culture, to be different.

"Nothing much, just relaxing. What is new with you?" John politely uttered, a bit nervous. He could hear Ernestine dressing, with the sound of the zipper on her pants being closed.

"Is someone here?" Ron inquisitively asked, craning his short, fat neck toward the bedroom door. Not waiting for an answer, he continued, "Oh, anyway, man, I went to the market and got a bunch of groceries. Going to put a few steaks on the broiler tonight."

Whoopee, John thought to himself, as Ron picked up his bags left at the front door and moved to the kitchen, whistling some rock tune, then singing; this Ron character was in his own little world of noisy music – maybe he did hard drugs like a lot of the rockers, or used to and got reformed. He sounded so intense in the singing, eyes closed, pretending he was a Mick Jaeger or somebody important.

"How about a Pepsi or a beer?" Ron said.

"No, thanks. Ernestine and I are going to head out and get a sandwich in a bit."

Peering, Ron said, "Oh, her, she's here?" He impulsively smirked.

Ernestine scurried out the room, fingering her hair, apathetic, and said, "Ron, how are you?"

"Great," he answered, not even looking at her, then he scrambled to put all the food items away, before sipping his Budweiser. Ernestine searched John's face, her arms folded, unsure of herself presently, like an intruder in the apartment where an intense frolic had just taken place.

"You know what—?" Ron added, just as the phone suddenly rang, seemingly louder than ever, and John went a few feet to pick it up, grateful for the distraction.

"Hello… hello? Who's this? Susan?" The phone clicked off, and he stared at it as if it was a foreign object, then placed it back on the receiver. He put his arm on the wall and murmured, "My God."

Ernestine, from the couch, nervously asked, "Who was that?"

"No one, really. The voice sounded familiar." He moved toward her, head down. "I believe it was this Susan Swanson I went to school with."

"Is she white? I assume so, since you went to that fancy college." She was peeved, concerned, and confused. She continued, "How did she get your number, John?"

"I don't know," he responded, perturbed, rubbing his eyes. "Maybe she called my mom's house, thinking I still lived there, and she gave her my new number... I hate her for that."

He recalled this student, Susan Swanson, a fellow Sociology Major along with his other friend, Anna Cohen, a Jewish girl; they called themselves the Three Musketeers, as they were always together on campus, studying for two years to make the grade, and graduate with honors. They were always delving into books, sharing ideas, values, and goals for the future; they were young, idealistic, full of energy, in the late seventies, when college was important, and the government was giving out scholarships for those students who had a high GPA. It seemed everyone from high school was planning their career, picking out several colleges to apply to, able to choose a major that they felt would push them to the top. Education energized John and his friends; there was nothing else to think about as parents pushed their children to enter its environs. This campus these three students chose, UCSD, was prestigious for the time, nestled in La Jolla, and the buildings were hidden behind huge pine and rhododendron trees, comprising of four colleges, large, grey granite buildings, huge lecture halls, two outstanding libraries, a large practice field, gymnasium, bookstores, and vast parking lots. These three people had an innocent relationship, and no serious feelings surfaced: it was all about the prize of education and knowledge.

Susan Swanson was a short woman with straight brown hair parted down the middle and small brown eyes. These eyes always stared at you seriously, but friendly. She did have a great smile that made her eyes wrinkle, and you could be amazingly comfortable with her. Her body type was bulky. She took people at face value and did not pass judgement rashly on anyone. Her demeanor was peaceful. Her clothes, though, were just put together as if she had no extra money to buy fancy attire, and she had not a care in the world.

After the quarter was over for them in the spring of 1981, John decided to celebrate with these two friends and get pizza and beer at the local hangout, the Rathskeller, on Muir campus. It was the place to be, always full of noise and the energy of young students talking, debating, delving into books and materials, or eating sandwiches and fries between classes. It tended to be a dark, dim-lighted place, with two levels, and a bar recently added for those who wanted to imbibe.

John walked into this place one late afternoon, the semester over, the meeting planned with his two friends, very relieved that the blue book essay tests were finished and feeling they had passed and done well. At the noisy doorway, John espied Sue and Anna already at a table, bent over, talking. They saw him and waved him over. As they continued their close conversation, he sauntered up to the wood table.

"Hey, guys," he said shyly.

"Sit down, John, and grab a beer," Anna demanded. Anna Cohen was Jewish, with kinky black hair, a pale, thin face with blue eyes, tall, thin, and she had this bad habit of smoking, and constantly playing with her hair as if distracted and uneasy. She would smoke and blow it out, closing her eyes: a ritual, as if she was imitating a famous movie actress like Greta Garbo or Marlene Dietrich. She lived off-campus with her wealthy parents somewhere in upscale La Jolla Shores and drove an older version of a BMW she got as a birthday gift. She tended to be shy around strangers, guarded, reticent at times, but very loyal in friendship. She was driven to succeed.

"Well, fellow Sociology students, cheers," Susan announced, lifting a beer mug.

Anna drank listlessly, scanning the club, her beer half empty. John quickly ordered one.

"You look a little tipsy, Susan," he commented.

"Who, me? Why not? It's over. I hate studying; I am trying to forget the routine, all the reading and work... the madness."

"How many have you had?" he probed like a doting mother.

"She had two already," Anna interjected, trying to palliate Susan's drunkenness. "If you don't slow down, you may never graduate. You drink too much," she asserted, shaking her head, eyeing John for validation.

Susan had a snicker on her face, guzzled her beer, ordered another and said, "Anna dear, you don't have to worry about me. I can handle my liquor, and I'm twenty-one."

"Then why are you almost falling out of your chair?" Anna added, disappointed.

Susan just laughed uncontrollably, with her eyes closed. John stared at her laughing, thinking she was crazy. He tended to be lenient and forgive her since they all worked so hard this semester with all the demand to read books, or parts of them, run to five classes each week on alternate days, and go to assigned study groups to get prepared for the impending doom of the final exam, write essay or term papers with footnotes, and, in general, run around the large campus with its various activities and sporting events.

"What are you guys going to do on the break?" he asked, his voice elevated due to the crush of surrounding noise.

"Nothing but sleep," Anna said calmly, "and forget this college; regroup for the next semester... Hey, I'll see you in that Political Science class; that should be a real bore."

"Yeah, but you need it towards your degree," John replied, shaking his head, staring at Susan Swanson, who was slumped in her chair, face red and euphoric.

"John," Susan inquired, slurring, "do you have a crush on someone, anyone on campus? You must, a nice guy like you, tall and all, you must have a secret girl. I bet you do, you suave dog." She trailed off in a giggle, still drinking, still silly as can be, as John was shocked. "A real ladies' man, that's what you are."

"I told you, I have no one serious yet. I am just a student right now just trying to make it." He stopped, dwelled on Ernestine, and added, unsure, "I did tell you about Ernestine, remember?"

"Oh, yes," she replied, her face lighting up, now erect in the seat, "yes you did, you said she was a good girl. She is black?"

"Yes, she is. She treats me right," John added confidently. "In fact, I would not trade her for anything."

Susan paused, staring through him, and said, "That's nice." She continued to drink, then became a little annoyed, using a few curse words to describe some of the professors and the educational system that was keeping her down and in her place. John shifted a glance at Anna, who moved her head forward and gave him the thumb sign to get Susan out of there before she could do any more damage or say something surly.

"Hey, let me walk you back to the dorm, sleep it off," he calmly suggested, his arms on the table, his head forward towards Susan. Anna continued to be silent, just staring in pity at her, arms folded, and embarrassed. "Come on, what do you say?" he said.

"Listen, lover boy, Musketeer," Susan said, her hands up, "I'm fine, really, just great. Hey, Anna, did you sign up for that History class with that old fart Pomeroy, or whatever his name is? He's a square, I have been told, who puts people to sleep. He must be in his seventies, and real boring. Oh well, I guess we must endure him next semester." She stopped finally, her beer finished. Anna got up and was leaving with her hefty backpack, and this was his cue to hoist the drunk girl out of her chair.

"John, Susan, see you soon," Anna said pleasantly. "Thanks for all your help this year, it means a lot to me." She then left, waving a hand back at them, and disappeared out the large door up a few steps.

After Anna left, John said, "Are you ready to go?"

"Go?" she said, offended, huffing. "What's the rush? You just got here." She glared at him in idle distrust.

"Let me finish this beer, okay, and we will take off," he placated.

Susan, after a moment, chimed in loosely, "You know what, John, you are becoming stodgy like dear old dad. One thing I give you is you are really dedicated to school, got a sharp mind, and too many morals for me; but, in general, you are a nice guy. Me, well, that is a different story. I take life as it is. I do my classes, and pass the grade, and have fun. I do give in to hang-ups like dear old Anna, who seems to be perfect and upright all the time, giving me lectures on what to do, how to act—"

"That is because she cares about you; you've known her for a long time. I would do the same if I had someone in trouble."

"Trouble, what trouble? Because I am a little tipsy? I will forget it happened by tomorrow."

"It is not just that," John asserted. "Your behavior has changed; you are a bit more aggressive these days. Is everything all right, personally?"

"Why of course, dear Musketeer. I have never been better. Life, you know, is stressful, it always is, and we must just deal with it. Drink up, finish your beer," Susan ordered. John finished his mug as Susan downed a tequila brought to the table, and right after that she slowly finished her beer while looking at John.

"Let's go," John ordered. Susan got up, wobbly at first, and she was escorted back to her dorm not far away, talking idle nonsense about politics, the campus, her family, anything that came to her mind. They went up to the fourth floor of a tall building, found her small room, she went in, looked back, and said, "Thanks, see you soon. Hey, listen, I have two tickets for movies at the Strand. Want to go?"

"Sure," he said, got the time for the show on Saturday, told her he would pick her up around six o'clock, and departed.

That cool May Saturday arrived. At five o'clock, he left the condo he shared with his mother and brother, telling her he would be home around eleven. She waved a goodbye as he exited the door and gave him a suspicious look.

He drove the red Plymouth to the campus and parked in a stall as night began to set in. He trotted up to the gray edifice, entered the elevator and pushed the fourth-floor button. He went down the narrow hallway made of concrete and knocked softly on the door and waited. *God*, he mused, *I hope she is not a mess*. The door was opened slowly as Susan craned her neck around the door edge. "Hello, stranger, glad to see you."

"Ready?" he said.

"Ready as I'll ever be, but first…" – grabbing her brown hippie-type bag with flowers on it – "I want to apologize for last week. I was out of control and embarrassing. You must think I am a lush."

"No, not at all," he calmly replied. "You just got caught up in all the festivities. I did not think twice of it."

"You are kind for saying so." She stopped, pondered, and went on, "You are a good friend, the best. How long have I known you?"

"Seems like years," was the adroit comeback. "Let's go catch that flick. I heard that the first one is a rag movie with girls with big breasts trying to seduce men."

"Well, what is the complaint? You will likely drool over that one."

He did not respond to that. They headed out to the Strand Theatre located at the beach. The Strand, an old, decrepit place was the hangout for students and hippies at that time. They catered to B-grade and countercultural films since the area it nestled in was this pot-smoking, rebellious youth neighborhood: hippies and bikers all around, time passed back to the sixties, rules were not adhered to, and the cops tended to avoid or overlook certain crimes, while vagrants lined the streets, and even sex acts in public were accepted. The Strand Theatre was to close years later to make room for retail stores. It did have the notoriety of being a controversial place to be, with all these movies of violence, sex, hints of sex, drugs, and anti-authoritarian genres catering to the rebels. The building had a white façade overhang that listed the title for the week. It was a small place with barred windows on the second floor, and they sold tickets for a few dollars apiece.

Driving on Highway 5, nearing the exit to the Strand, John looked over at Sue Swanson. He studied her for a brief second, trying to gauge her mood. She was happy and calm. He asked, "After college, what do you want to do? You said you may want to teach."

Shaking her head, she replied, "I'm not sure at this point. I'm a little hung up on what to do, what jobs there are out there. It's a little scary and overwhelming... I may go back home to my parents' house after it's all over. It's hard enough just paying the bills on the campus job I have."

He understood, nodding. "Where are the folks living? San Diego?"

"No; of all places, New Mexico – Albuquerque. It's so hot out there, you can't breathe in the summer. They have a nice three-bedroom home. My mom said if I ever needed to come home, the room is waiting. I don't what to do that, do you?" She appeared deflated.

"I understand your fears. I live at home, that's my story. My parents are divorced. I told you this before. My crazy brother is there, too. We won't talk about him. I plan to take any full-time job and move out of that dungeon as quickly as possible. I hate it there. Always under the thumb, scrutinized, rules to follow, stale. My mom is a piece of work."

"You don't get along with her?" she said, surprised.

"It is not just that. It is hard to explain, but it is too tense there. I am twenty-two now, soon to be twenty-three, and it is time to make it on my own. There is no privacy there with her snooping into my affairs, worrying constantly, and any time my brother leaves, or acts out, it destroys my peace of mind. Those two can have each other." He stopped his tirade.

"My parents, devout Christians, have been married for almost twenty-five years, and they never seem to complain; they are so compatible, it's scary, and I wonder if married life is like that. My dad is successful in business. They are so supportive of me."

"I wish I could say that. My dad, he has good qualities, but one fault is he is so critical of me. Everything I try to do, he complains due to his lack of success and insecurity. He is an educated man, but he really lacks poise and wisdom. My mom is different; caring, but overprotective and manipulative... Let's change the subject."

She understood and put her hand on his shoulder as he parked the car in a free space on Abbott Street. She said, "I hope I didn't upset you... about the family?"

He stopped the car, and sternly answered, "Forget it. Let's go."

They both got out of the red Scamp, and John, for some reason, became nervous. He was on a real date with Susan, the first time, away from campus, with no Anna in tow. He questioned his motives and mood. Would Sue be friendly? Would she desire more? He thought of Ernestine, who he had been dating for about two years and he did not tell her of his plans. He told her, instead, that he was going to the ballgame with Brad, his best friend, and would call her Sunday. That was reasonable, he tried to tell himself: innocent fun, no attachments, and no expectations. He felt sorry for Susan when she was drunk at the Rathskeller, and the depression she exhibited. He kept fighting these two dual urges to have an enjoyable time with the college chum and stay faithful to his girlfriend Ernestine. He, for a moment, regretted accepting the invitation to the movies, but the tickets were free, and he did not want to hurt her feelings by declining; besides, he needed a break from the routine of life and his girlfriend.

Moving to the front door of the theater, John did not hold out his arm to her, so they walked apart quietly. He had the image, suddenly, of meeting Ernestine in that theater, irrationally believing she may have even been following him, and he quickly dispelled this fear from his mind.

They entered the theater and went through a small double door to find a seat. He bought some popcorn at the concession stand and passed it over to her. She smiled, said thanks, and became excited with the upcoming movie, the young crowd talking and muttering in the aisles, people laughing, the lights still up, middle class folks, rebels, people with long hair, sideburns, and goatees, wearing faded blue jeans with thick belts, biker boots, or buckled shoes; the women, too, dressed in flare pants popular at the time, with long earrings, funky bright-colored shirts with puffed sleeves, a few girls with afros, a smattering of black girls with white girlfriends, giggling, some with tattoos on arms and backs, several geeks with glasses, in checkered shirts, by themselves with no dates and with other guys in their early twenties. This was the crowd, that day, at the Strand during its romantic heyday. Everyone was relaxed, no one cared or made judgements of anyone here based on race, appearance, or gender. John, before the show, scanned the entire theater, the stage, the aisles, and dwelled back several years ago when he took a young blonde woman Downtown to see a B-grade movie from his county job he had part-time while in school. It was so impulsive! He must have been eighteen at the time, watching some ludicrous movie about the beach scene and all these girls in it, laughing, always carefree, trying to promote this stupid Hollywood image of the good, white life, with privilege, the young men living at home in expensive mansions owned by their parents. He recalled, unfortunately, while the movie was playing in these wooden, partition seats, seeing a 'roach cross over on the adjoining rail by them, wondering why he was dumb enough to take a date to this place. He was limited on funds, and she, Julie, did not care. The movie screen was a bit blurry, and the sound cracked every so often, still they were insouciant, and when it was over, they grabbed a burger and milkshake from a takeout restaurant. He took her home to her parents' house, kissed her, and never went out with her again.

He pulled himself back to reality as the curtain went up on the show; the muttering stopped for the most part, except for a few, immature couples in the back that had imbibed too much and were told by their neighbors to shut up. This movie, *Beneath The Valley of the Ultra-Vixens*, starred Uschi Digard, known for her soft-porn movies and magazines. As they watched, they discovered the whole tone of the story involved big-breasted, Anglo-Saxon women attempting to seduce and have affairs with desperate, groping men. It was all so stupid, crass, but no one seemed to care, and they continued to watch the contours of these women and hopeless, ugly men in the potboiler that went on for ninety minutes, and when the lights went up, John and Susan, glum, shaking their heads, decided to leave and not stay for the main feature. John took a deep breath, secretly aroused by the voluptuous women in tight outfits with their foreign accents that he had just seen, but he was unsure what to say about the rag movie to his friend. Susan did not seem to mind, and with a placid face she said, "Mm, good movie." She began to softly laugh.

John responded idly, "What the hell, it was a cheap thrill." That was all he said, and while exiting, he, for some reason, wondered who Susan Swanson really was: he had known her for a period of time only at school, and did not know her past, what drove her. Did she ever have a boyfriend? Was she experienced in bed? Did she believe in God? Probably not, as she was such a surly rebel, who was deep down anti-establishment. Many of the college students at the time were defiant, against the arcane culture trying to dominate everyone. He was too afraid to delve into her past, her fears, her desires, and her motivations.

They got into the Red Plymouth and pushed through the endless crush of traffic down the main beach street, driving past endless bars, smoke shops, antiques stores, a market, liquor stores, small businesses, and banks, heading out into the night to drive back to the campus dorm. The ride was pleasant, with small talk on school subjects, as Susan leaned her head towards the passenger door, and then switched to his shoulder as he pulled into the dark, dimly lighted parking lot on campus around nine o'clock. He parked, turned off the engine, and said gratefully, "Thanks for the movie. I appreciate it."

Susan looked searchingly at him and rubbed his arm with her left hand. She impulsively reached out and kissed him on the cheek. "There," she placidly said, "you needed that. I know I did. I wanted to do that for a long time, but was afraid…"

John straightened up in his seat, rigid, confused, yet slightly flattered. He was not attracted to Susan, not his type, and Ernestine was lingering in the shadow of his consciousness.

"You needn't have done that. Thanks again for everything. I'll see you at class in a week," he asserted.

Susan, in a trance, continued to rub his arm, as if she may pounce on him at any moment or flee in fear. It was like she had taken on a different personality and changed to something demonic and forceful. He was not sure what she would do or what he should do. For a second, he dwelled on pushing her out the passenger door in derision. But she opened the door, got out, bent low to look at him and said, "You are the one, the catch. Keep me in mind. See you." She then left, walking quickly to the entrance of the building, and disappeared inside the glass door.

John stared at the entrance, his breathing heavy, and he decided to call Ernestine first thing Sunday morning.

# CHAPTER 2

John Earley came out of his reverie in the apartment, after the strange phone call from Susan Swanson, and faced Ernestine, querulous, on the couch. He sensed some deep trouble or resentment if he could not explain himself and this silly antic from some girl who, for all she knew, might want to frolic in John's bed or already had.

"I really don't know how she got the number. I don't even know what she wanted. She just said 'This is Susan', and rudely hung up the phone."

"Just Susan, are you sure? Are you dating her on the side? If so, let me know so I can get the hell out of here and move on! We just made plans to get married, and you have this bitch calling you. Sounds strange to me!"

"Well," he passively continued, "it isn't anything to be concerned about. I have not talked to this woman in over a year since college. She said she was leaving and going back to New Mexico to live with her parents. Hell, this is strange to me, too."

Ron Miller, the roommate, left the kitchen area, waving his hand. "See you guys later; going to take a nap." He shut his door gently.

"And I don't want this aired out in public to your roommate or anyone," she annoyingly commanded. "No one, got it? You need to set this chick straight if she calls back! If you don't, I will!" She became agitated, her tone increasingly elevated, eyes wide, arm flaying out, glancing fiercely at John, with her lips closed. "You better take care of it, quick!" she added.

John, crumpled on the couch, troubled, sweaty, eyes down, did not regret studying with Susan at college. He regretted going on the silly date last year. It was meaningless. Did Susan want to go further with him? Was she stewing all this time because she was rejected? Would she call again to harass him? For all these questions he did not have an answer to this quandary. What he realized, presently, was that he needed to be tactful and supportive of his girlfriend's wishes and feelings, or everything would come tumbling down. He fervently wished to resolve and end this situation and friction.

Ernestine inhaled deeply, now composed, her hands together, and she blurted out, "Do you still want to get a sandwich?"

"Yes, sure. Listen, Ron can tell you that this girl has never called before or showed up here. In fact, no one has ever been in my apartment since we started dating." He was emotional and struggling with his message. "If she calls again, I will take care of it. For all we know, she may be calling long distance from her folks' house or was drunk and calling as a prank."

He searched her face after his speech. She seemed appeased, grabbed his arm, and said, "Let's go. I don't want to talk about it any more."

They got into his car, and John scanned the parking lot to see if Susan was in the gold Plymouth Duster she owned, if she still had it. No Duster was to be seen. They drove the short distance up the street and ordered two torpedo sandwiches at the deli. While they were waiting, an attractive Black woman with a weave sauntered in front of them. She was buying a soft drink as she passed, and she scanned them up and down purposefully, with a smirk and scowl, as if they were museum pieces. Ernestine, askance, looked at John to see if he was ogling her shapely figure. He was not; he just looked ahead at the menu over the counter. The home girl paid for her drink, passed them, and made a disapproving face as she left the store.

"Take a picture why don't you!" Ernestine rudely said, as John tried to calm her by patting her arm. The Black girl just kept walking to her car.

"What's the matter with you?" he said.

For a moment she was silent, angry, and responded, "I don't expect to get treated like that from my own people, especially from that whore."

He was shocked she said this, seething still from the phone call, he surmised. He quickly got the sandwiches from the shocked clerk and went outside to eat at a table with a shade. Not much was said while eating, except the gist of the conversation was: she better not catch his white ass chasing other women.

It was a long, dreadful fifteen-minute drive back to Ernestine's clean, mid-century apartment. He pulled up to the long driveway and rambled down into the back of the two adjoining houses. She looked intensely at him, sighed, and then gave him a kiss, saying, "I have to work the day shift tomorrow. You have a spare key, come over tomorrow around five... and give me time to get over all of this, okay?"

"Okay, honey, whatever you say. I'll see you tomorrow."

She got out, not looking back, and climbed the long wooden stairs on the side of the garage and entered the unit. He sat there a minute and decided to visit his mother since he had no plans, and it would take his mind off his problems. Maybe mom, for a change, would have some answers and be supportive. He debated telling her of the engagement and decided to postpone the announcement due to today's strange phone call from Susan Swanson. *Susan*, he mused, *what the hell are you doing calling me, saying nothing, and hanging up? What do you want to say?* He drove in a fog, shaking his head, frustrated at his life now, this friction developing that had needed never to happen. *Thank God I didn't stare at that beauty in the deli with her delicious figure in the tight jeans, putting on a show for me, and then having the temerity to stare us down in hatred.*

He arrived at the condominium complex not even remembering any of the trip there, and parked in one of the spaces on the side of the building. It was his father's old space, now gone, divorced now for three years. He refused to dwell on this and the pain. He slowly went to the condominium door and rang the doorbell. His mother Anne Earley opened the door with a pleasant half smile.

Inside, guarded, he asked her how she was doing. "Terrible," she admitted with a grimace. "Your brother is gone again, who knows where, all night and all day, he just leaves. He says nothing. He thinks this is a hotel."

"Does he have a job?"

"He says he works part-time in sales."

"I heard that before," he emphasized. "Really, he needs to get his own place if he can't follow the rules and grow up!"

It was as if his mother did not hear what he said, was in her own misery. "I'm so afraid at times," mom replied, frowning, ready to whimper.

"Stop, stop that. That's not going to help or change the situation. He is okay; he is putting on a show for attention."

"I wish I could believe that, John, it's terrible living like this." She almost began to cry halfheartedly. "I don't know what I can do. Can he stay with you?"

"Are you crazy? I don't have the room, and if I did, I'm not going to support him and his bad habits. He drinks coffee all day, and wonders why he is up all night prancing around; and I heard he has the nasty habit of smoking. Forget it, he needs to take care of himself."

"If that is the way you feel as a brother… no help; well, I can't change your mind."

"Listen, mom, the guy is twenty-one. You need to kick him out or give him an ultimatum about what is expected of him. You can't baby him forever; it will kill you." He said this fervently to give the last pitch to the disturbed mother about what to do.

Mom did not seem to listen, or care, and stood idly in the living room deep in thought and her face was red. His mother was now fifty-four, still attractive, standing at five feet five, with sandy brown hair, a large, aquiline nose, and if you saw her picture when she got married in 1958, you would think she was a princess, a Grace Kelly type. Her only health problem was this nagging arthritis she always complained about to people, grabbing a hand to prove her point in the telling. But all her charm and dreams fell apart after three children were born in the early sixties, and the father, Joseph, angry, dominant, unable to sustain a job, all the firings, terminations, and quitting made his mother a bitter woman. It simmered over the painful years into a loveless marriage that ended in 1979, with his father packing up his belongings into the 1973 Plymouth Fury monster car and disappearing to live in a small apartment in the mid-town area to get away from all the suffering.

"Has anyone called for me recently?" John nervously inquired.

"Oh yes, let's see… an Anna, an Anna Cohen called two days ago."

"Why did you not tell me?" he asked, annoyed.

"I forgot to; with all this trouble with your brother, it slipped my mind."

"Do you have the number?" he asked in anxiety.

"Yes, over on the table. I saved it for you. She said it was important."

He told himself it could be about Susan, since they stayed connected with each other. He trembled slightly, took the small note with Anna's number and added, "Mom, I will see you later. I must run some errands."

"Can't you stay? Making potato pancakes."

He shook his head. "No. I'm going out with my girlfriend tonight" – lying and evasive.

"Oh, Ernestine," she ruefully remarked. "How is she?" She did not care for an answer, turning her head.

"She's great, still a nurse... I really like her," he said in defense of her, and to set up the time for the announcement. "We are going in the right direction, everything is perfect."

John's mother said nothing for a few seconds, arms folded; then, "Oh, that's nice." She moved away to the dining room, fixing place mats and the flower bowl on the Spanish-style table. John was perturbed and confused by her mannerisms, her quietness, the frigidity of it all.

"Bye," he said, turning away in disgust and leaving the condo monastery. In fact, the whole, short visit was a waste of his tim;, he concluded that he had, and will always have, second place to his brother, and this constant warfare where he and his mother had to assert their rights, their viewpoint, and his mother could not bend an inch, especially when it came to him, his girlfriend he loved, and any other area of his life not really important to her because she was trapped in misery, confusion, and endless anxiety. He thought this was all useless, needless, solvable if only she could take the steps to fix the issues in her life; and his father, too, when he lived here, had the opportunity of making amends, striving for a solid career, spend time with his children and complain less in general. These two were like barking, fierce dogs, always ready for the attack, for the pounce, and looking for any opening to hurt the other with a surly remark or action.

He drove up the hill like a maniac to find the phone booth to call Anna. Dear old reliable, quiet, mature Anna, he thought, her voice always soothing, reassuring, never raised in anger. He veered around a few cars, made it to the top, and swerved right into the gas station. He skidded to the phone booth; it was the same one from which he called Ernestine two years earlier, while he was living at home, desperately looking for a date. That day was forever seared in his memory, now present, and he jumped out of the auto and ran to the booth, dialing the number.

"Hello," the voice quietly said, polite.

"Hello, Anna?"

"Yes... is this John?" was the lively response.

"Yes, how are you?"

"Fine, great. Hey, guess what. I got a job as a teaching assistant in Sociology on campus. I start the next quarter."

"That's great, you deserve it. Are you pursuing a Masters?"

"I'm thinking about it. I'm staying with my parents temporarily until I find an apartment and save money. It is good to hear from you."

"Listen, my mom said you called. Anything wrong?" he asked.

"Well, yes. This sounds strange, but a few days ago Sue called me, upset, out of sorts, and asked me to go to her place in Clairemont. She is renting a room in this dirty old house."

There was a pause, so he prodded. "And what happened?"

"I got there, and she looked terrible, nervous, upset. Her room was messy like she had a fit and threw everything around. It was not like her to be that way. She said some odd things. She said she was upset with you for spurning her – that is the word she used, spurned, so direct and angry."

John, in the booth, opened the door for air, playing with his shirt collar. "That's crazy, we just went out on one date… let's see, about a year ago. Is that what she is upset about? She never mentioned it in class or ever after that. Why now?"

Anna placidly said, "I don't know. She looks like she is on something, a bender. She said, also, she wants to get even with you."

There was an intense hiatus to process this event. "Even?" he annoyingly answered. "Even for what?"

"I don't know. You could call her—"

"Damn! I don't want to call her; I want to forget her if she is going to act this way!"

"I called just to let you know, warn you," she carefully responded. "Does she have your number?"

John, unsure, replied, "Yes, that's the problem. Out of the sky blue she calls me, says her name, hangs up, with my girlfriend sitting right there on the couch. How do you think I feel? Damn, it's annoying when I get accused of cheating on the side. Susan needs to move on and get some help, real help."

"Sure," Anna pleasantly answered. "I agree; she needs to move on and not be so obsessive." She then switched the conversation. "How are you faring? How is the girlfriend?"

"I can't complain, life is good. And do you know what, we just got engaged. I can't believe it myself; I was a nervous fool proposing down by the beach yesterday. Of course, she said yes."

"That's wonderful. You deserve each other, and from what you told me about her, she seems wonderful and your soulmate. Will you invite me to the wedding?"

"Of course," he stated, happy, confident. "As soon as we pick a date, I'll send you an invite. What's the address?"

Anna rattled off her parents' plush La Jolla address and he wrote it down carefully, repeating the numbers and street name.

"John, it was good to hear your voice. Remember the slogan, 'The Three Musketeers'?" she animatedly asked.

"Musketeers, one for all, and all for one – of course I do," John responded. "Listen, I'll talk to you soon."

She said goodbye and he hung up the phone, wiped his mouth, turned around, stared at the neighborhood for a minute, and went slowly to his car in deep thought, face furrowed, hands in his pockets. He sat on the comfortable cloth seat and stared out the windshield.

# CHAPTER 3

As her fiancé pulled slowly out of the driveway, Ernestine opened the curtain and watched him slowly back up and move towards the street. She was on the side of the curtains, by the edge, so he could not see her. She had a tear in the corner of her eye, sighed heavily and said, "Gosh, I do love him." She recalled the phone call by the woman and decided she had overreacted; if he said it was nothing, then nothing existed. After all, he pledged his love and honor day in and day out, never wavering, never straying. He did propose – oh so nervous at the beach. What more can you ask?

She saw him just a little bit different now. She tried to compare him with the old boyfriend Spencer and concluded they were two different men. Spencer was abusive, continued his heavy drinking, and would meet women on the side to have affairs: he was so careless in his love, hiding out, dodging phone calls, saying he was in one place, then another. He had an angry tone to him, even put his hands on her to hurt her. After all of this, over three years, she decided to call it quits and sever the relationship. Later, he tried to call her a few times to rekindle his love, but it was fruitless; when her mom told him that her new boyfriend was white, he became enraged, used racial epithets, and asked her why she would settle for some stupid white man. She did not respond to his questions and would hang up the phone on him, eventually changing the number. To her now, he was a stupid, classless man with no real ambition who did not know how to treat a lady because he had no father or role models to educate him.

She felt better after processing this. The phone rang, she did not answer. She wanted to continue the peace of her day off before she went back to Sharp Hospital tomorrow to start another demanding shift. Ernestine Jones was, after six years, a good, resolute nurse, polite, efficient, rarely upset with demanding patients in their pain and confusion. She had a few admirers at the twelve-floor glass hospital, one a nurse named Rico Lombardi, Italian, a strong-looking man with slick brown hair who always made jokes and remarks to her and asked her out a few times. She refused him, telling him constantly that she was in a relationship; it was finally accepted, but he spent time searching her voluptuous figure in the tight white outfit on occasions when together on shift; she sensed his presence and leers out of the corner of her eye and did not say anything about it, because it was silent, quick, and not followed up with touching. She did feel his stare, and those of others, and tuned it out in her busy day of dispensing medication, checking charts, changing endless linens, conferring with nurses and doctors, all of it demanding and crucial. She was well paid in this prestigious hospital that had been growing with increased funding since the mid-fifties.

She decided, today, to do nothing. She scooted to the bathtub to turn the water on and relax in a long, steamy bath, with lavender soap. She then turned on the radio to a jazz station, grabbed some wine from the fridge, filled the glass to the brim, elegantly with gusto, and, eyes closed, she sipped the Chianti. She carelessly removed her clothes in the living room, drew the blinds and went to the bedroom. She climbed into the tub, sitting in total ease, one toned arm on the side of the cast-iron tub, and took another draught of the wine before beginning to wash herself.

A half hour later, she got out of the tepid water and put on some skimpy pink panties, a loose t-shirt, and cotton shorts. Moving to the window, she felt euphoric. *Gosh*, she thought, *I'm getting married!* Finally, the struggle to find a soulmate was over; it was a new chapter, a new life with this suave, soft-spoken man. She dwelled on his toned physique, curly brown hair, the stubble on his face before shaving, soft and playful, those turbulent green eyes that see through you, and his strong hands when he held her. She moaned slightly, her eyes half closed, and drifted off to sleep.

A loud knock was heard on the main door on the side of the kitchen. "Hey, sis!" was shouted.

Ernestine cursed, adjusted her clothing, rubbed her eyes, and opened the door. Her young sister, Brenda, was there with a cigarette between two fingers lowered at her side. "Put that out!" Ernestine demanded as she moved back to the living room.

"What's happening, sis?" Brenda said with little effect.

She was told to sit down. Ernestine became excited, and when Brenda was next to her on the brown couch, the music still softly playing in the background, the wine now loosening her tongue, her hand on her toned leg, she stated, "Well, you are not going to believe this. John and I are engaged... Can you believe it? I'm finally going to get married!"

"Hey, great. I like John, he's cool." Brenda, the younger one, was twenty-four, not as pretty as her sister, an inch shorter, but she still had the family trait of the narrow face and cheekbones. Her hair was in a short brown afro, she was a chain smoker, and employed at a retail store up from the house she shared with her mother. She could be caustic at times, saying exactly what was on her mind, was known for a few catfights with girlfriends, and associated with lower middle-class Black men who tended to be in trouble, or just got out of trouble or jail. Brenda barely graduated from high school and did not pursue college. She was happy and resigned to celebrate, drink, occasionally smoke pot, and have young men fondle her either in cars or rooms in nearby houses where she lived. She did not care what people thought of her and her ways. She led a secretive life, and old mom, now in her fifties and heavy set, was in her own world watching endless television shows and re-runs in her chair, with crossword puzzles, working part-time, and receiving alimony checks each month; in sum, she did not keep a close eye on the younger daughter's activities.

Ernestine continued, "He made the proposal at the beach. What do you think of that? That is the best place to do it, to me. I am so happy right now, like a release of energy. He has all the qualities I have been looking for. He's tall, handsome, goes to church—"

"And has a nice body, mm!" Brenda archly added. "I would like to meet me one also."

Ernestine playfully patted her arm. "You keep your eyes and hands to yourself."

"Sure, of course. I would not want to ruin perfect bliss." She giggled. She probed, "The main question: are you going to tell mom right away?"

"You know, girl, I think I will, but it is better said in person, don't you think?"

"I agree," Brenda said with emphasis. "Something like this, and white, you better tell her straight up, at the house."

"White, white," Ernestine responded, annoyed. "Why does everyone get caught up in that? Hang ups, dumb, stupid hang ups. Look, he's not different from any other guy really, and add in a college education, a regular job, and a Christian, what could be better? White… I'm so sick of hearing that."

"Me," Brenda said with assured emphasis, serious, "I got me a man, Dwayne; he treats me right." She was competitive in the telling. "He works, has a car; who knows, I may tie the knot some day. How about a beer?"

"Get one from the fridge," Ernestine answered, pointing her finger. She went on, "This Dwayne, he's no good for you, take it from me. He's like that has-been Spencer, a player, loose, on the go. You should hook up with someone from our Baptist Church."

"Church? Are you kidding me?" she said with a frown, insulted, guzzling from the Miller Beer bottle. "No one wants anyone from that sterile, frumpy church with all those old geezers. When you were younger, did you see anyone there as a possible candidate?"

"Candidate? This is not a political office… this is about love, connection; and, believe me, skin color doesn't really matter."

"It matters to some, like dear old stodgy dad. When you tell him, he's going to flip his lid and give you a long lecture like your life is going to be hard."

"Wait, stupid," Ernestine interrupted. "That's the old way, the old school of thinking before all the changes. People who think like that are racist, ignorant, or in marriages that they can't keep together themselves, so how can they judge?"

She paused, lips closed for a few seconds, eyes up, then continued, "No, I'm not going to condone or fall into that trap. People are people, and you need to get past this skin color, high yellow, mixed race, mulatto, all these stupid, insane words that don't really mean anything. It's just categorizing people to keep them in their place with hurtful labels and racial groups. You know it's all so wrong."

"Ernestine, despite all that, I do support your choice," Brenda excitedly asserted. "When is the big day?"

"Not sure, we haven't talked about it. I guess tomorrow, after work, John and I will come by the house to talk plans and spring the news on mom. Keep it a secret until then, okay?"

"Lips are sealed," she stoically responded, sitting forward, sipping the cool beer, now smiling, and admiring her sister with her eyes.

"What are your plans for the rest of the day?" Ernestine asked.

"Not sure. Got any chips?"

"No," she said matter of factly.

"I'll probably go home and change. Then call Dwayne. Might head out to the club tonight."

"The club, again. Aren't you getting too old for that tired, low-class joint on Imperial Ave? You can only get yourself in trouble over there."

"You are just stuck up and frumpy. Ain't no harm going there for a drink," she replied acerbically.

"Oh, you know I'm kidding. I just think you should make better choices, plans, meet some nice, wealthy gentleman."

"Wealthy gentleman? Where? Where we live, hell no, there aren't any wealthy people, as you say. The type there is limited, and you are lucky to find a guy who isn't hooked up with some chick or has three kids already. I wish I could find one." She trailed off and was preoccupied with her thoughts.

"Whatever, it was only a suggestion," she replied with a straight face.

Ernestine switched on the television as Brenda became quiet, perturbed, mulling over the issue she had with meeting gentlemen. She was indeed trapped in her own life and thinking limited her choices, professionally and personally, to what she was exposed and comfortable with. Ernestine realized she was silent now and reflecting as they continued to watch some movie.

Fifteen minutes elapsed, and Brenda downed the last of the suds, got off the couch, and said, "Got to go, sister. Congrats. See you tomorrow."

She scuttled out of the apartment, a little tipsy, the door was slammed, and she was gone. Silence. Thoughts. Plans. Ideas entered Miss Jones's head as never before: reception, where? Limousine, type; wedding ring, diamond; church, ceremony; garter belts, fun; marriage license, line, invitations, who to invite; all of these new terms were all so vital, so final, to pull off one of the biggest weddings ever seen on Tanner Street, where her mom lived.

Brenda mentioning her father was a crucial force in her wedding: he would be giving her away, and respect needed to be shown. She was still attached to Jerry Jones, although gone now for fifteen years. Where did the years go? She presently tried to focus on his good qualities and less on the proverbial faults mom always mentioned. She recalled, fondly, the day, when she was eight, and Brenda five, that dad packed up the Chrysler and moved out of St Louis. He told them he was tired of the freezing weather and crime, and mom agreed to move west to California as their destination; he stated he had a defense job prospect in San Diego. He planned everything, he sold the old, small, two-bedroom house, arranged the furniture to arrive at a certain time in California once he found a rental, took care of all financial business, and on one sultry hot September day he put everything he could carry into the large sedan, with a roof rack, put the children in the car with sandwiches, and headed out of the city early one morning. Her mother, about twenty years ago, was livelier and more attractive, with a short, cropped hairstyle like Elizabeth Taylor; she had light brown skin, wore an immaculate dress, fashion shoes, and looked like she was dressed for the theater. Dad warned them on the long trip that would take three days not to throw up in the back, and not kick the back of his seat while driving. He took with him a large map and he looked at it often to make sure he was taking the right highways. He was like a sea captain staring at it, his finger pointing to routes and exits like he was navigating a big ship. He even had mother looking and telling him where to go and turn. The trip gave everyone a chance to see the country, stopping for food and shakes at Howard Johnsons; and Ernestine, even so young, remembered going through a northern part of Texas in a town where all these white folks stared at them from their porches. Dad just kept going at a high speed, looking neither to the right nor left. They, she recalled, passed through Arizona, and at the time, at dusk, the temperature was around ninety degrees, and Jerry for a moment thought of living here since it was quiet, but the heat deterred his decision. The trip went on and on, and they arrived in San Diego one cloudy morning to stay in a hotel. Shortly after that, they located a three-bedroom house in the middle of the city, the place prior to the one on Tanner Street. This was Ernestine's journey, and she wasn't sure why it entered her head, but she relished the easier, happier times with her dad.

The phone rang, and this time she picked it up in premonition. "John," she pleasantly said, "I'm glad you called... What? You, too... Well listen, honey, I'm sorry for earlier today, just jealous. I know… now, I need to trust you unconditionally. I'll see you tomorrow, right?" She was anxious.

"Of course," he astutely replied. "I miss you already. Can't wait."

"Listen, here's the plan. After work, we are going to my mom's house to tell her the good news. Are you fine with that?"

"Of course, it's your mother. We need to get this out of the way. I know we will have her blessing."

"Let us hope so. My sister was just here, and I told her the news and said to keep it quiet until mom hears it."

There was a short pause, then John breathed into the phone. "I was thinking, short notice, can I come over and spend the night?"

Joyful, elated, she replied, "Of course! Bring a subtle change of clothes. Tomorrow is the big day; you can hang out here until I'm off from work."

"Right. I will be there in an hour."

"Bye, honey." She hung up the receiver. She got more wine, drank some, went to the couch, one arm over the side, shaking her elegant head, and, smiling, she whispered, "When you get here, Johnnie boy, you are going to get a nice, nude surprise."

# CHAPTER 4

"Ron, what's new with you? I haven't seen you all week," John said, this late Saturday, on the couch, as his roommate Miller was drinking an iced tea, leaning over the kitchen counter, the bright sun coming in through the large window behind him.

"Not much going on. Working overtime at the warehouse," he placidly said, no effect, almost lifeless, eyes tired. "Eric and I – you met him – we are going to the rock concert tonight."

John paused, thinking his roommate was lonely, never with a girl. Ron Miller was short, with brown hair parted in the middle, running to his shoulders, with a round face and developing a stomach at twenty-eight. He had been living forever in the apartment complex, posting an ad in the *Reader*, and John happened to respond in time since the old roommate skipped out on the rent. He was interviewed by Ron at his apartment and was told he would contact the manager to add him to the lease, only he needed to complete this one-page application, which he did, there, the same day, and John moved in within a week. He said goodbye to his mother, glad to finally leave, and couldn't believe his luck in finding this spacious two-bedroom unit with a vast living room, on the corner of the building. John brought his spare items with him, including a color television to add to the décor, and bought a used double bed from Amvets. Over time, John noticed that Ron was always in his room for extended periods of time, implanted deep like a German soldier in the trenches. Then he would burst out of the room and say, "What's the haps, man?" This was his opening line, and John did not know what to make of him or what was his passion. Initially, he thought he was home often because he had no money, and later realized that he must have very few friends and was a recluse.

"Are you going to call that Vietnamese girl?" he almost pleaded. "She sounds like a wild one."

Ron stoically stated straight at him, "I am not sure about her. She seems too much to me, aggressive... she is too short anyway."

John mused, *Gosh, what other choices do you have? You are young and you should be out dating and taking chances.* He was afraid to tell him this. He commented, "Ever think of settling down, getting married?"

"Me, I guess. But you know what, I believe you need to have a good credit score of at least, let's say, six-fifty, and two thousand in the bank before you settle down." He sounded so distant and stupid to John, who stared at him in amazement.

"Oh, really," John rejoined. "I think you should find the right girl first, keep working, plan, and save later."

Ron, unmoved, shook his head. "I don't think so at all. You need to have a good financial base first."

"If you believe that, then you need to quit that job of yours and get into the stock market or real estate to make all the money you need. What about that?"

"Reasonable, reasonable," Ron answered, thinking, wondering about John's motives for saying this. "That makes sense, but not everyone wants or can be a tycoon or money chaser; that's not me. If I really wanted to be rich and famous, I would pursue a music career playing the electric guitar. You don't mind if I practice with it in my room?"

"No, that's fine, just not too late at night," he responded, getting tired of talking to him.

John Earley just sat there in pity as Ron moved to the kitchen to put the glass in the sink. He peered out the window, turned around, and said, "There is this gold car out there; it's been parked there forever, all day, in the corner stall by the trees. What the hell?"

John got up to look out the window. Ron wanted to call the manager; he was famous for always complaining about something around the complex and was a clean freak. John stared out the window intently and saw thirty yards away a gold Plymouth Duster with a woman in it, the window almost rolled up. This person was looking ahead of her, leaning forward on the steering wheel, and then she turned her head to scan the building. Quickly, hands closed, determined, John flew out his door and went down the steep steps of the complex and approached, carefully, the dirty gold car with a slight dent by the back fender. He squinted about ten yards away and saw Susan Swanson in the vehicle, one hand on the wheel, glowering at him, lips pursed.

He shouted, "Susan! Susan! What are you doing here?" He was just a few yards away from the vehicle, the engine running, and she quickly backed up the car towards the exit, almost hitting him in the leg, and he quickly veered out of the way. The Duster and mysterious Susan just sped off, making a screeching sound in the lot, turned right on the street, and left. He listened to the car noise until he could not hear it any more. He stood idly in the parking lot, heart beating fast, and looked up at the apartment. Ron was still there, craning his neck to the glass, watching the scene. John turned around, pensive, and went up the steps back to his apartment, not sure of what to make of Susan or what to say.

On entering, Ron, still in the kitchen, asked, "Who was that maniac? Do you know that chick? She almost ran you over," and he nervously laughed, cursed under his breath, and awaited an answer.

"No, I do not know her," he evasively answered. "Must be some prowler or homeless person looking for a spot to park."

"Whatever. If she comes back again, I'm going to report it to the management. She may be casing the building."

"Sure, that makes sense," John answered, distracted, annoyed with his roommate, who was always acting like a busybody; if he had a real life and outlet chasing women, none of this would bother him, and his expression of hate and revenge now was a little silly. John thought this to partially distance the incident that just occurred, seeking to bury it forever. He went to his room, not looking at Ron, who now moved to the living room.

John grabbed his duffel bag, wallet, and keys on the dresser. He left the apartment, waving to his roommate, who maintained silence in the living room, and closed, carefully, the front door. He started his car, looked around the lot – no one was to be seen – and exited. He did, indeed, need to get away, remove the depressing roommate, the weird phone call, now Susan hanging around for no reason. Surprisingly, while driving, he put it out of his mind for now, and dwelled on what the wedding would be like. As he continued to drive, he thought about his fiancée, with her short, black hair that he adored; he kept repeating her name: Ernestine, Ernestine, Ernestine Jones. He liked how it sounded and rolled off his tongue. Ms Ernestine Jones, nurse. He was proud of her profession; she was an accomplished young woman who was going places. He said to himself, *Nothing else really matters. I am the lucky one to have found this diamond in the rough*; and the garbage and pain in his life was lessened for the moment. "She is such a cool girl," he said as he neared her apartment.

He reached Cleveland Avenue and parked his car on the street. He quickly walked to the back of the house, skipped the steps two at a time, and rang the doorbell. He waited, and there was no answer. Puzzled, he hemmed, fumbled for the key, inserted it, and entered the apartment and the dark kitchen. He carefully said, "Honey, I'm here." No answer, all was quiet. He became worried. He moved to the living room and found Ernestine, on the couch, in skimpy red lingerie, her legs crossed. She seductively said as he stood there, "Hey, stud, it's about time. I have a special treat for you."

She rose from the couch and went towards him, grabbed his neck, and passionately kissed him. She started to stroke his arms as she removed his shirt, breathing heavy, scanning every inch of his frame. He let her do this, as he dropped his bag on the floor, cupped her face, then kissed her neck, fondling her.

"Strip, come over here," she demanded as she moved away from him towards the couch, removed her panties and bra, knelt, and leaned her stomach over the edge of the couch. She beckoned, "Come on. Make love to me."

John frantically removed the rest of his clothing and went over to the eager girl, and began to rub her neck, back, and her firm behind. Ernestine's eyes were closed, as she leaned her head back to him. To him, she had never looked so beautiful and desirable. The blinds were drawn, the music was off, and no noise could be heard in the sleepy neighborhood. John grabbed her hips and made slow, passionate love to her. Ernestine, with her head on the side, mouth open, grabbed John's left arm in their ecstasy, then she nuzzled his neck to wildly kiss him. He felt good to her, the strong arms around her sides as they continued their passion. John felt the smooth skin, inhaling the lotion and lavender soap scent keenly. When it was over, he laid side by side with her on the couch, necks and bodies together, stroking each other in silence.

Shortly later, she inquired, "Do you want a beer, babe?"

"Sure, I do need one," he gratefully replied.

Ernestine got up, and John's eyes pored over her as she wiggled with her dark, Aphrodite frame to the kitchen to get the beer. He knew she was perfect, flawless to him, this day, and every day. They were both still nude and so comfortable with each other, and they explored their bodies guiltlessly, without shame. She returned momentarily with two beers, her arms pushed tight against her body with the long, noticeable fingernails.

"That was nice, real nice," she asserted.

"Yah," he quietly said. "I was so surprised when I came in to find you in that red lingerie I like. Were you planning all of this?"

"Of course. I got to treat my man right. I sure got your attention." She scanned his firm, muscular frame, the messy brown hair, and his intelligent green eyes. Then she glanced at his private area as she handed him the drink.

"Cheers," she continued, composed.

"Cheers," he responded as he took a long gulp of the fluid. She sat down next to him on the couch, sipped her beer, put her hand on his shoulder, studied him, and possessed him with her eyes. A few seconds later, he continued, "Tomorrow is the big day. I hope she is in a good mood."

She responded, "Just be on your best behavior. I do not want any issues. What clothes did you bring? Mom likes a clean, well-groomed man like my father was, and no foul language," she lectured.

"I brought what you told me to bring: a clean, cotton shirt, dress pants, thin brown belt, loafers, cologne, toiletries. I'm the total man."

She laughed at this last remark. They both got up to put the clothes away as Ernestine straightened out the living room area. John went to the cabinet to find a snack. They were in quiet, comfortable unison, jovial, as if they had been living together for years and understood each other's movements, mannerisms, and secrets.

"Let's take a shower together," she suggested, pulling him towards the bedroom. He patted her behind and she was receptive to the touch and smiled. The shower was one of the few private moments they loved to do together, without noise, without the phone, without racism, without the problems of a complicated, harsh world. It was their chance to explore and revel in each other's body and appreciate its pleasures. They began to soap each other down, as the steam enveloped their frames, washing, rubbing, quietly talking. John always admired Ernestine's magnificent figure in these moments: her perfect breasts, toned tapered legs, tight, subtle arms, and her smooth skin with no blemishes. Ernestine, too, was enraptured with John's tallness, his defined pectoral muscles, bulging thighs, and she began cleaning and rubbing his hairy chest, washing his curly brown Italian hair, stroking his backside, and playing with his extension again in the long shower. This was their snippet in time, intensified by the marriage proposal, and nothing could touch or break them: no institution, no family member, no ideology, no class, or group, no one could interfere with their destiny; it was unshakeable, not to be altered, and to be revealed. They talked about this and searched for role models for validation. If Antony could be with Cleopatra, then they could do it. If Sammy Davis could marry Swedish actress May Britt, they could do it. If Leslie Uggams could have a fabulous marriage and be with Grahame Pratt for years, they could also. She knew that this John Earley had a journey, too, and had come a long way in the three years as a student at UCSD. She molded him into the man, at almost twenty-four, she wanted him to be: assured, unafraid, and free. She also had a journey to complete: to rid her past of the abusive boyfriend she dated, time wasted in a relationship that was going nowhere but destruction. She, with effort, had to sever ties with some of the ghetto, Black people and ideals that were outdated and fading away. All this before, and now this day, was reinforced in their coupling and commitment. No one could be against them if God was for them.

They both got out of the shower and dried each other off. John slapped Ernestine's round behind and pulled her towards him. She said with an eyebrow raised, staring over her shoulder, "Like that?"

"You know I do."

"You best not forget it!" She moved away, and added with two fingers raised close to her eyes, "And you better keep your eyes on me."

He half laughed and scanned her as if she was a prized possession. He, the dreamer, went into his past and recalled, as a young high school student, that he began to stare at Black girls in the streets and magazines catering to dark, exotic beauties. He was fascinated and enamored with the dark skin tone, believing they came here from some foreign land to tease him. He found an easiness, a forbidden aura in them. In college, he was searching for an identity as he was searching for knowledge; it wasn't enough to understand books and ideas, it was crucial to finding his niche, what his tastes were, what women would be attracted to him without conventions and rules to follow. He wanted to be accepted for who he was: a quiet, reserved, and misunderstood man. He was left-handed, the middle son, Catholic, an introvert, and these qualities tended to distance him from the crowd and people he knew. He liked the soul scene: he listened to music by Diana Ross and Roberta Flack; he watched, secretly, movies of voluptuous Pam Grier, stately Eartha Kitt, and debonair Leslie Uggams. He increasingly became mesmerized by the dark, sultry faces, Black and tanned-skin women with high cheekbones, braided hair, flashy looks from models like Beverly Johnson, weaves, hooped earrings, the language inflection, the fashion styles, the cool clothes, the toughness, the forcefulness. He liked the total Black woman. At his job he had many close Black associates and played basketball with the brothers at the court, who, over time, accepted his good playing skills.

"Hey, honey, let's eat some chips at the table," she suggested. They finished putting on shorts and shirts and moved to the small round table in the cramped living room. Ernestine sat down, facing her fiancé, looking straight at his green eyes, and fixed his hair while stroking his arm. Her narrow chin was cupped in her hand, elbow on the table. She started, "So... what church shall we pick? Baptist or Catholic?"

"You decide; either one is fine with me."

"I'm thinking about your mom. How about your church?" she spat out, the chips chewing in her mouth.

"Sure," he hesitated. "I will ask my mom to set it up; she's been going there for years and knows the monsignor."

Pondering, she suggested, "Should we plan it out over six months? I think that would be enough time to make all the arrangements."

"Yes, sure. We need the time to save money; who knows how much everything will cost. I want it perfect for you and to show everyone that we are in love. By the way, who is the maid of honor?"

"Probably Jeannie Cooper. I've known her since high school. She will be so excited about it."

"I don't know about her," he cringed. "Do you even think she likes me? She seems to avoid me and is not friendly."

Placating him and touching his arm, she said, "Oh, sure, she's fine with it. She likes you in her own way. Give her time."

He shook his head. "Jeannie, every time we see her, she does not give any eye contact with me, and hardly talks to me. I don't call that friendly. I think she has an issue with white."

"No, she is just shy. If anyone has an attitude towards you, they will hear it from me. I won't put up with it."

This Jeannie Cooper was about the same age as Ernestine and was a cautious girl living down the street from her in her father's house. She slept in a bunk bed with her brother in the other room and worked at a county office. She wore thick glasses, and had coffee-colored skin, was attractive in her makeup appearance, and had a fake laugh on occasions.

John added an afterthought, "I think Jeannie would be cool."

*Cool, cool, cool*, Ernestine reflected. *He uses that word loosely, and all the time. I guess that is the word of this beatnik generation. She thinks I am so cool, too; I am glad of that since he thinks I am so hip. John could be in the middle of Harlem, by himself, and not care because he likes everyone, and accepts people for who they are, no pretense, no judgements, no acerbity. He is comfortable with the street folks, he works with them, Asians, Mexicans, Filipinos, all of them enveloped in the various pockets of the town. He told me when we first met that one of his best friends in middle school was this guy named Vitasi, a Filipino, who lived across the street from him. They did everything together, went to school, played stickball in the street, went to the movies down the street, and when Vitasi's family relocated, he was crushed. He was crushed because he was loyal, and when John finally let you into his world, it was final and forever. His friend said in testimony to him in his yearbook, and it went something like this: 'John, the one thing about you is that you treat everyone with respect. Good luck in the future.'* Ernestine decided, and knew, that this was his essential nature.

"Hey," he annoyingly said, "wake up, what's wrong with you?"

Composed, now she continued, "Who is the best man? Brad?" she insinuated, calmly.

"Yes, Brad, who else would I pick? He has stuck to me through the tough times. I would not trade him for the world. He is like a brother to me."

"I am glad you feel that way; he is a good guy with a sense of humor, a bit of a loose cannon, though."

Brad Markinson, also a graduate from a different college, was six one, with a receding hairline, even at twenty-three, and had the traits of a perpetual smile and charisma. He was popular with his friends because he had a forceful personality and styled himself as a ladies' man, at least in theory. He had, on occasion, a fiery temper, and no one knew what mood he would be in. He tended to be a prude and dated only blonde girls: he talked blonde-haired person, dreamt blonde, and desired blonde. His clothes were carefully pressed designer shirts and pants, and he would not tolerate anyone who was poor and didn't meet the mark.

"I agree with your choice. I think Brad is steady." She recalled the time they double-dated, and Brad had this blonde girl at a fancy steakhouse called Bully's, and she kept ordering and guzzling glasses of red wine before and during dinner. She became tipsy, and Brad became enraged, sitting across from her, staring at her with him mouth-opened with food, not believing what he was witnessing. Of course, the bill skyrocketed, as Ernestine and John had only one drink apiece, and small portions of steak, and they were both uncomfortable with Brad going on and on castigating this girl named Nicole. After the meal was finished, everyone said a quick goodbye outside the restaurant and went home. Any double-date dinners were put on hold for a while after that.

Ernestine Jones now was truly in her own place, catching her own stride after thinking about this incident. She was comfortable in the so-called white world because it was the place that gave her things she desired: money, fashion, a nice 1980 Ford Mustang, perfect diction, perfect etiquette, fancy Shakespeare plays to attend on the weekends, white girlfriends to boost morale and status in the rich, old money world; connections to wealth, goods, events, chic parties to put your name out there – in sum, to crave and obtain the best things in life. Her first and only old boyfriend, Spencer, Black, was a distant memory. They did have good, precious moments, but over time it dissolved as he became distant, abusive, and he began cheating on her. This flawed person made her deeply resent Black men. It severed her connection to them and the ghetto forever, this hard world of cheating, deception, no social movement, babies out of wedlock, men having a problem with the law, and no marriage proposals; this pool of men, for her, was limited and pushed her in other directions. Some other family relations, too, were lost to drug use, divorce, or unemployment.

"Now that we got the church out of the way," John practically added, "what is next on the list?"

Ernestine thought for a moment, as she chomped on some chips, her jaws moving quickly. "There are so many things to do, sort out... What about a limo? I want a really nice one."

"You got it," he animatedly asserted. "I have this guy at work, he's Persian, and his father owns this Mercedes limousine company. He said if I needed anything, just ask.

We were talking one day, and he told me due to all the conflicts in the Middle East that no one liked him because he's Persian and people are afraid he is a terrorist or someone in his family is. Isn't that stupid? He said people address him as 'those Iranians' in a surly tone. We laughed it off all the time. He is a super guy."

"I didn't think the Persians would have so many problems in this country like Black people have," Ernestine commented, shaking her head and exhaling.

"Well, they do. People must always find someone to hate and make fun of. Isn't that the way of the world? Hatred, distrust, avoidance from a bunch of unhappy, uneducated people who can't see past their own face."

"Anyway, you are a super guy. You like everyone. People feel comfortable around you. That is a good trait to have. I sensed that about you the day I met you. I said to myself now here is a guy I can trust and relate to. I don't know how I felt it, but it was there. I guess it was the goodness deep down in you that people feel. Sounds silly bringing this up, again."

"Not silly, honey, at all. You are not so bad, either. You have a nice disposition and your elegance, the way you carry yourself was what attracted me to you. How could anyone hate you?"

"They do," she immediately said. "Just look around this town, look what's happening in the country. All the dumb stares we get. Even though we are a sharp-looking couple, it does not mean anything to many folks who can't get past color. It's so stupid, honey, but true. Look at that bitch in the deli when we went to get our sandwiches. We did nothing to her, but she gave us the cold shoulder and stared us down!"

"That is because she doesn't have a man. Too many jealous, insecure idiots out there. We can't change everything and people's nature. We can't."

"Yes, anyway, limo. Check. What's next?"

"Well, the big one, the reception hall. Some people just show up for that to feed their faces and get drunk."

"Maybe my Baptist Church by my mom's house. They have a big hall there. It's an old place and my parents used to attend the services there." Jerry and Earlene Jones: what happened to them in time? Some of these secrets about the parents she presently kept to herself to be revealed later. Her father, always there nagging at her, all six foot four of him, with his wide handsome face, perfect teeth, wiry, strong, confident. She remembered an old black and white stock photo of the family: mom, pretty, sitting in her short dress, and plastered black hair, and the two brats in the photos, babies around four and seven. What happened in time? Ernestine even felt she had a hand in the demise of the Jones family beginning in the sixties. It all went down a dark abyss of despair, distrust, and the falling away of love due to drink, other women, unruly children, and large bills to pay to maintain the standard of a three-bedroom house. Eventually, her father moved away to live with a floozie – that's what her mother called her – a gold digger, to Arizona, now gone fifteen years. It didn't seem right, and it didn't seem possible to Ernestine that her father would leave the nest, but he did. John's father did the same thing, too; it was common to all races and ethnicities that certain core problems and feelings transcend race. Now she was stuck with a depleted, older mother living on a fixed income, and a younger rebellious sister who couldn't see past her passions. At this moment she was determined to wipe all of this away, bury it, in matrimony with a handsome man who would take care of her and dispel the dysfunctional forces being imposed on them. John vowed, he said one day long ago, that he would never wind up like his parents were when he tied the knot; this was his vow. Nothing, she concluded, would destroy or separate them.

"Hey! Wake up! I asked you a question," John uttered in annoyance. "Where do you want the reception? I don't think your church will do. People may not want to go over there."

"Why not?" she inquired.

"Unfortunately, a lot of my side of the family may not want to because they are stuck up."

Pausing, perturbed, arms now folded, she said, "They may need to get over it. This is my wedding... my church, your church, all the same. It depends on the church cost. We are not going to put up with any rude troublemakers. They can stay home for all I care."

John was quiet and shrugged his shoulders. He said, "Why don't we put off the rest of the details for another day and enjoy ourselves? What do you want to do?"

She grabbed his neck and pulled him close to her face and replied, "I want you all to myself. We need to cherish these moments. Let's get some food, make popcorn and watch a flick tonight."

He agreed, and they moved to the couch. Surprising him, Ernestine suddenly asked, "Any more phone calls from that woman?"

"No, none," he calmly said. "If it happens again, I will deal with it." He kept the car in the parking lot a secret, now and forever.

"Good," she pleasantly said. "If she comes back again, I will kick her ass. I'm not going to put up with that."

John just stared ahead at the television.

# CHAPTER 5

Susan Swanson awoke early Sunday morning in a fog. She had disturbing thoughts while sitting on the edge of the bed, her hair disheveled, and she looked worn. She had a dream, or nightmare, that she was at college, going down this long hallway, where she met a professor about school; he told her that John or someone like him was in the building. She kept moving down this long hallway with all these doors, but could not find him. Then she awakened, alarmed, huffing, and in a terrible mood.

She got up and put on some worn, faded jeans, a white shirt and tennis shoes. She opened her door, looked down the hallway and no one was to be seen or heard. She had rented a room from the owner at an affordable price. She had been living in this old three-bedroom house since graduation, and the owner, a female, was always at work. She had only a C average from school that continually tortured her, knowing she could have done better if she did not have such a debased nightlife. She began screwing students on campus and would meet them at their apartments to do lines of cocaine, loosening her inhibitions. She became a slave to her habits, was late to work often, and people stared at her as if she was crazy or handicapped. She did not care; she tuned everyone out who would not give her a fix or cater to her needs. She became a debauched fool.

John Earley was on her mind now for her next conquest. She was determined to rekindle her relationship or friendship, despite his feelings for his fiancée. She would not even believe that he really had a fiancée because he was all hers, in her thinking. He was too young to settle down with some chick from across the tracks; she refused to believe she was right for the handsome student she remembered. She recalled the date at the movies, as she insidiously, secretly wanted him and his body all to herself. She would not let go of this thought, and it recurred repeatedly when she was in the mood. Even now she feared her close friend Anna Cohen might be moving in on her territory, disrupting. Yes, John had a crush on her, and she was probably dating him.

She moved towards the kitchen and dialed Anna's number that she kept in her purse.

"Hello, is this Anna?" she said softly.

"Yes, who is this?" was the terse reply.

"Susan. How are you? I haven't talked to you in ages. What is new?"

Anna, guarded, surprised at the early morning phone call, responded, "Nothing new. How are you doing?"

"Not too good. Listen, have you talked to John lately?"

"No, why? He is on his own, has his own girlfriend. He plans on getting married."

"Married... how rash. That is just like him to be so impulsive. So, you are not dating him?" she rudely asked.

"Dating? No, of course not. What gave you that idea?"

"Just a hunch. An attractive girl such as yourself, you never know. I would like to have him to myself and won't stand anyone getting in the way."

"Sue, are you crazy? Are you smoking something?" Anna hinted, a little nervous.

There was a short, awkward pause. Susan stated, "Anna, darling, of course not. You know me, just a little pot to get me through."

Anna Cohen saw this sign in the last year of college with her and John together. Susan became distracted away from her studies and was seen less on campus, she didn't talk about books, or courses, or goals; she seemed to become a hedonist, desiring to drink beer and indulge in men's company. She became jumpy, afraid, and unable to concentrate at times, and at other times she was totally focused; she put assignments and papers off to the last minute, and on the night before due, she would cram and write furiously to make the deadline. She did not tell John, or anyone, her desire for him, growing into an obsession. John was too determined to graduate to notice or care if any girl was after him romantically. He had been dating Ernestine so long that Susan was not that important any more or in the limelight of his thoughts. After graduation in 1982, John did not call her or contact her at all, believing she would relocate somewhere to begin a career.

"All right, Susan, what do you want from John? You should just leave him alone," Anna asserted.

"I wish I could. I find him very desirable; that's natural enough. And you know what, I don't believe he is getting married to that chick. Who is she anyway? A nobody."

"She happens to be a genuinely nice person, and don't go and spoil things. My advice to you is to move on, and work on the career you were talking about. You said you wanted to get into counseling, didn't you?"

"Maybe, maybe not. There is plenty of time for that. I must just tie a few things up first. Anyway, Anna, I must go. Bye."

The phone was hung up and Anna was insulted, wondering what she meant about John, dating, and keeping him to herself. It made no sense. Was she joking? It was not like her to be this way, Anna brooded. She sensed some trouble ahead, or at least Susan Swanson was fated to have a total breakdown. Usually a calm, decisive person, Anna was unsure about things, the conversation, the meaning behind the phone call. She debated if she should call her friend John to let him know this, but she did not want to intrude on his peace, his happiness with Ernestine. She searched for an answer, her brows lowered. After several minutes, she decided to go out and shop at the local mall down the hill in La Jolla, a new strip mall catering to expensive items and wealthy clientele; her parents supported her with an allowance each month, until she began her new position on campus.

After the conversation, Susan intensely dialed John Earley's phone number. The roommate picked up the line, said hello, and she hung up. She cursed, unable to hear John's soft voice, and became agitated, thinking he was hiding out and avoiding her. *What is there not to like in me?* she said to herself. She decided, impulsively, to drive over to his apartment, park on the street and go knock on his door. She was determined to settle things, and to let him know of her affection. She was driven to this action to express her desire for him, begin dating him, rekindle their romance, and she refused to believe he had a meaningful relationship with some Black woman. Over and over, she told herself it was a lie, an absurd ruse to throw her off the track.

Susan banged open the front door to the house and walked a short distance to her car, and with trembling hands she put the key in the ignition and started the rumbling car. She reversed the car quickly, almost hitting a person crossing the street, and drove the gold Plymouth at a high rate of speed. She inhaled some controlled substance on the way.

In a few minutes, she was veering in and out of traffic, the car heading east toward the rising sun. She was talking to herself, cursing, and yearning to be with her pseudo-lover. "John," she asserted, "you know in your heart you want me; you can't turn me down, we have been through too much together. And I can show you a fun time if you give me the chance." She was wantonly silly, vague in her thinking, not making any sense. On the drive, now, she was smiling, dreaming, the drugs ingested taking effect. She was high and she did not care.

Susan did not remember how she made it to the complex. She parked her car under a tree just outside the complex and she was able to view the window where John lived. The distance was fifty yards away, and Susan sat quietly in the car, mulling over what course of action to take.

Suddenly, a man, about thirty, with glasses, came up on the passenger door and knocked. Susan rolled down the window. The man, with a surly face, stated, "Hi, I'm the manager here. Just to let you know you can park your car here all day. I got complaints from the tenants that your car was in the visitor space all day. I am warning you not to do it again."

Susan, frazzled, said, "I am not harming anybody. What business is it of yours?"

The manager hesitated, offended by the remark, and with both hands on the car door he said, "Please, miss, move on. If I see the car in the lot, I will have it towed. Who do you wish to see here?"

"Just a friend I went to school with. That is my business, not yours."

"I am not going to argue with you. Just remember what I said before I call the police!" The irritated manager left the car and walked back to the manager's unit and slammed his door. Susan glanced up at the corner unit where John lived and saw no activity. Seething, staring, and glaring at the manager's unit, she started the car and headed back to her house.

# CHAPTER 6

Sunday morning finally arrived. It was early at five, with a developing cool mist outside enveloping the building. Ernestine rose, with a sigh, from the warm bed to go to work: she looked over at John with a smile, asleep, buried in the covers. She rubbed his curly hair and got up to dress. The coffee was on a timer, and the scent pervaded the room.

This was Ernestine's quaint apartment: it was shaped in the form of a U, recessed from the street and snuggled between two houses built during World War Two. It overlooked a garage, and to enter it one had to go on the side and climb several steep wooden stairs to enter it. Once inside, there was a long, narrow kitchen, with a huge cast-iron sink, a small fridge, and an old, decrepit gas stove and oven. Going to the main part of the house, there was only enough room for a tiny, glass table and chairs, so clean and unused to denote the dweller ate out often. Immediately to the right was a large brown couch, with floral prints, abutting the main living room window that looked out into the driveway and street. In front of the couch was a classy cabinet where the color television rested, and on the opposite wall was a bookcase that contained ceramics, pictures of her family, and a few volumes of books, including *Anna Karenina*, Jane

Austen's *Pride and Prejudice*, *Native Son* by Richard Wright, and Marilyn Monroe picture books. The bedroom was small, barely fitting the full-size bed, one large oak dresser, and a few framed prints of black models in poses. The adjoining bathroom was immaculately clean; the total apartment smelled fresh with some room deodorizers permeating the air.

She donned her nurse's uniform consisting of white pants, a short-sleeve blue shirt, topped off with a white hat. She mumbled, "This is so white, but I got to make that money." She sighed and continued to dress, putting on a faint Anne Klein perfume and a slim leather watch. She adjusted her hair, put on some makeup hurriedly, looked in the mirror, shook her head in approval and snatched the car keys on the dresser.

"Hey, sleepy head. Got to go. Be here when I get off shift; should be home around three." She talked fast, pawed her watch, gulped the coffee, and added, "I have some eggs if you want to make them."

John was awake, rising, looked at her at the bedroom door and approved. "The total professional nurse," he grinned as he nodded. He added, "Babe, I'll be here checking out the games."

"Later," she said, kissed him on the lips, and left the quiet, cold apartment. The 1980 white Mustang two-door she treasured was parked inside the cramped garage. She backed out carefully, the jazz blaring on the radio, and headed south on Cleveland Street to enter the highway and the short distance to Sharp Hospital, a few miles north. She got there in ten minutes, parking the sporty car on Frost Street and went to work in the multi-story glass-framed hospital built in the mid-fifties. This building had about three hundred beds, was prestigious, and growing. Ernestine was glowing and happy today as she entered the double doors to work.

As she greeted people with pleasant good mornings, she was dwelling on her mother, and she made the rounds of patients, some in pain and complaining, and other older folks just sitting listlessly in their beds with televisions blaring. She checked charts, consulted with nurses and doctors, dispensed medication, changed dirty linen for incontinent patients. This kept her busy until eleven o'clock, when she went on her break, grabbed some tea, and decided to go to the seventh floor to get a view out of the vast window of the horizon that went west to the sea. She just stood there in contemplation and at peace, carefully drinking the hot fluid.

Ernestine Jones, the classy, cool girl was really at the center of this story; she was the catalyst, the vortex of events that have already occurred and will occur. Her strong personality demanded it so. She thought about her interracial relationship for a moment; she knew in her soul that what she and John had no one could touch or emulate. Their love, she averred, was so strong, too assured for the naysayers or unhappy individuals that so wanted them to fail because, by doing so, they could keep the *status quo* and validate their unhappiness. She wasn't sure why she thought about this: she may have had some fears of disapproval from family members and friends she loved and trusted. She presently, at this moment, at the time of her engagement, did not want to deal with or accept negative rude behavior.

In the early eighties, people were reaching out past race, past guilt, past religion, past norms, to form bonds of new friendships and marriages. The movement started the fire, at it would not be until twenty years after this tale opens that Black and white couples would be accepted by the majority. People now, young and old, with energy and boldness and disregard of the arcane institutions and values, were crossing racial lines to find solace and love in a changing world. Mexicans were living with whites, East Indians were marrying Pakistanis, Jewish girls were finding Catholic men, despite the forces of religion, Indians were with Chinese, Irish were mingling with Sudanese women, Russians were with Bolivians, Haitians were with whites, and Persians were finding mates outside of their culture. All these groups were striving to rewrite history, dispel myths, of what is right and wrong and normal, and accepted, erasing fears and their own misgivings to forge ahead, in courage, and find soulmates, because the old order was decaying.

Ernestine continued to stare out the immense window, in the partial gray sunlight, the teacup in her right hand.

"A penny for your thoughts," a voice said behind her.

Startled, turning around, she saw six-foot Rico Lombardi a few feet away with a stolid face. "Oh, you startled me," she rasped.

"Sorry, you looked like you were a statue," he concluded with a smile.

"You know me, just trying to catch a break from all the insanity You are on a break?" she quietly asked.

"Yep. So, Ernestine, what's new? I haven't seen you in a while." He stood there, tall, muscular, one of the few male nurses in the hospital with his perfect moussed hair, olive skin, clean shaven and dark curly hair.

"I have been around," she answered evasively and carefully. His look made her uneasy.

"Would you like to have lunch?" he insisted, peering close to her.

"No, I brought my own," she lied.

"No problem," he said with a pathetic smile, with a fake grin. He delved, "Say, what's out there?"

"Nothing. Just thinking about life. When you look at this window with the beautiful view, you can't but help to wonder about things: life, God, plans."

"How's the boyfriend?" he asked directly.

Ernestine wondered why he would ask this. She appeared a little offended, taken off-guard, unsure what to say. Did he think that if John wasn't around, he could move in and try to pick her up? Rico, to her, was too friendly, nosy, and forceful. "He is great," she said, not mentioning the proposal because she did not care what he thought, and he was just an idle man who happened to work with her. "He takes good care of me," she added, her face assured.

"Gosh, I wish I could find a woman to take care of me," he stupidly uttered.

"You got to go out and find one, a good girl."

"Where?"

Ernestine pointed at the window. "Out there, in the real world. Not some stupid hospital. All the nurses here are overweight or married."

Rico Lombardi stood there, stolid, processing what she said. "You mean take a chance, date anyone?"

She was not sure what he meant. Rico Lombardi, for all his talents and arduous work, was missing something; she concluded that he lacked grace, poise, and was not able to meet and carry an adult conversation with a woman. "Anyone, anyone will do," she asserted. "Take a chance, find one; it's not the person you may plan to date, but reach out. I've known you for three years and I've never seen you with a woman or talked about one."

He swayed his head, eyes briefly closed, and responded, "I go out. I certainly don't find dates in this hell-hole. I just can't find anyone at the bars that I can relate to." He sounded so helpless and inept, making excuses for not finding the right woman.

"Well, Rico, I know you can do it if you want to," she added.

He stood there silent, a few feet away from her, and said, finally, "Ernestine, I guess you are right. I need to widen my horizons."

She became annoyed with him, and responded, "Listen, Rico, I got to go back. See you soon."

She left him there in the lobby. He stared out the window to avoid looking at her, and Ernestine, with his face turned, did not have to gaze on his sad, defeated face. She shook her head in derision and she continued to move away to the elevator. Rico, Rico, such a sad individual. So many men, she mused, stuck in neutral, unadventurous, no chivalry, no courage to cross the abyss.

She finished her shift at two thirty in an anxious mood with John constantly in her thoughts. She ran to the car and sped to the highway back to her apartment. Presently, she had a pit in her stomach, not from the stressful work, but the pending meeting at her mother's house, with the announcement of a lifetime, so final, not turning back. She refused to look back, never would look back, never the old ways again, the ghetto world, Spencer, even high school companions, because she realized that if she went back, regressed, she would be oppressed in the heavy weight of despair and people's daily problems, and they would say: Oh, I can't find a man or woman. My husband just left me, what do I do? Can you loan me a hundred dollars? Do you have a spare room for my sister who just lost her job? I need a job; do you know anyone? Why do you have love and happiness and not me? What, he is white? She did not want to help and psychoanalyze anyone she knew that was needy, ungrateful, and unwilling to change and to see the truth and beauty of life right in front of them if they reached out to take it, take a chance on living, get rid of despair, depression, anxiety, and make something of this life. She truly did not desire to coddle people whose goal in life was to use you, and then turn their back on you. She hated friends who were stuck in misery, illness, and fear. For this woman, the only important things were her fiancé and a future.

She arrived at the apartment, entered hurriedly, and found John buried in the couch, beer in hand, half asleep, with the Padres's game on.

"Wake up!" she barked.

He looked at his girl in a daze, with his shirt off. "I'm ready."

"You don't look ready; get dressed," she insisted, shaking her head. Ernestine put her bag down on the chair.

She studied him as she walked to the bedroom and took off her uniform. "Give me a few minutes, I need to freshen up." She changed into some flare pants, a cotton shirt and white tennis shoes. She put on fresh makeup, brushed her hair, added a touch of red lipstick, and decided she was pretty. John came up from the back and gave her a squeeze. She smiled with her eyes closed, loving the strong caress, the kiss on her neck, his hands touching her behind.

"Move away," she commanded. "Let me finish and then we'll leave. Whose car?"

"Mine," he tersely answered. He did not look nervous. He had on khaki pants, a brown short-sleeve shirt, leather loafers, no watch, and a splash of cologne.

"Comb your hair, it's messy," she said.

"Looks fine to me."

"No, it isn't," she asserted, grabbing her brush. She combed the dark, curly hair for him, straightened his shirt collar, patting his stomach. "There now, you are set." She eyed his face, a bit red, and added with scorn, "How many beers did you have?"

"Just two, babe," he answered innocently.

"Don't have me check the trashcan. That's enough for now. Remember, you are driving."

He did not respond, but had a silly smirk on his face, and, in fact, he'd had three drinks.

There was frenetic movement in the apartment as Ernestine cleaned up his mess at the table, putting away papers, trash, clothes. "Just to let you know, if you are going to live here, you need to clean up. It looks like a bachelor pad."

"Sorry," he said with a fond grin, "I am in training."

She answered back adroitly, "As long as you are in training, that's what counts."

She snatched her handbag and pulled John toward the front door. She stated, "Here goes nothing."

While driving, John looked askance at her and said, "Do you remember the day, about three years ago, when I first met your mother?"

"Of course, how could I forget it?" She began to laugh. "You looked like a scared cat. Boy, you were smooth going in, but after that—"

"After that," he huffed. "What? I thought I was cool, nice, a gentleman – wasn't I?"

"If you say so."

"Your mom was just sitting in that old chair, and you introduced me, and she said, 'Nice to meet you, John,' with that big grin. I think I shook her hand like I was on a business deal."

"And don't forget those chicken sandwiches she made, just like you were part of the family, and she knew you for ten years."

"That was some day. You know, your mom is quite a person. She takes no guff from anyone, but on the other hand she would give you the shirt off her back if you needed it."

"I wish your mom was that way, a little more approachable," she added.

He was struck by the word 'approachable', and he thought all moms should be caring, forgiving, and direct. But Anne Earley was not, and he knew it, and nothing in this world would change that. Not a million dollars, or caring husband, or loads of friends; she was who she deigned to be, and she wouldn't budge. He continued after reflection, "My mom has come a long way in that time. She has issues, though; if she could just get rid of the hang-ups and my brother, she would be a lot better off."

"You're telling me," Ernestine agreed. "When are you going to tell her about us, the arrangement?"

"Soon, maybe immediately. Let's get through today first. Will Brenda be there?"

"I hope not, she's a pain. She adores you, but sometimes she is silly and stupid, and she may say something she may regret. Then again, she may even have some dude over at the house."

John digested this remark; some unknown Black guy to size him up, an intruder, a foreigner. He did not want that. He was still unsure of his place in her family and total acceptance to be placed with some man who would judge him, stare, and make snide comments. Then again, he could be a super guy or someone who did not talk much. All the near future was unsure, unsteady, and alarming.

"Whoever shows up," he surmised, "this day is about us, and I don't want any grief from some guy. If so, we will just hit the road."

"Come on, honey, it's not like that. You should not be so scared."

"Just being practical," he elegantly said. "Practical."

They drove on for several minutes, winding through narrow streets, John recalling that first day he drove to the house to see Ernestine and her mother. The streets, houses, people had not changed; it was still the same sleepy neighborhood of duplexes and older homes built in the forties. He tried to decipher the mood of people and their appearance on the street, but came to no conclusion except that they minded their business and looked like ordinary middle class citizens walking or working in their gardens.

Finally, they arrived at the house. John parked the car on the street, and Ernestine looked squarely at him, and said, "Ready?"

"Ready as I will ever be," he placidly responded. "Let's do this."

They got out and held hands as they walked up the driveway. Brenda was already there, smoking a cigarette.

"Hey, Sis, what's new?" Brenda calmly said, her eyes squinting with smoke in her face, the cigarette loosely in her hand at her side, as she stared deeply at the couple.

"I just came by to see mama," Ernestine replied, pulling John past her.

"Hello, John. How are you with your bad self?" Brenda remarked archly, puffing furiously in the air. Ernestine gave her a mean stare, opened the door, and found her mother in the kitchen.

"Mom, just came by for a quick visit!"

Mom was silent, reserved, her face looked tired, and she was bent over the sink, peeling potatoes. For a moment she said nothing, as if she was gathering energy to speak something pleasant and wise.

"Hello, John," she finally said, as he was standing around the corner, in the living room entrenched in the brown shag carpet. He wasn't sure what to do or say; he was waiting on Ernestine's cues. He decided to move towards the television and watch an old episode of *Gunsmoke* in black and white.

Earlene pulled Ernestine's shirt and whispered, "He was here yesterday."

"Who, who was here?" she responded, searching her mother's face.

"Spencer! You know who. He wants to get in touch with you."

"Shit, I don't want to have anything to do with that loser! I hope you didn't give him my address and new number." Ernestine was becoming upset, uneasy, and she had her hands on her hips.

"No, of course not," her mother said complacently. "I thought you should know. He seemed desperate and wanted to tell you something before he left."

"Left? Where is he going?"

"He said back to Chicago, since nothing was holding him here any longer. I'm not sure, but he could be fibbing."

"I wish you hadn't told me anything about him, because, frankly, I could care less. Whatever he decides to do, keep me out of it. I don't ever want to see him again."

Her mother said nothing and it seemed as if she was disappointed with her remarks about the old boyfriend Spencer. She turned around and continued peeling potatoes. Ernestine turned the corner of the kitchen and nervously stared at John in the living room, quiet and passive.

"Mom," she firmly said, "come into the living room. We have an announcement."

Mom, arm in arm with the daughter, moved toward the chair as Earlene had difficulty walking due to diabetes. She sat in her proverbial throne. John looked at Ernestine for a second, walked over towards the chair, and calmly said, "Mrs Jones, with your permission, I would like to have your daughter's hand in marriage."

The mom, with her wide neck craned upwards, immediately answered with a smile, "Oh, how nice! Congratulations to you both! When is the day?"

"We haven't picked it yet," Ernestine interjected, as Brenda entered the house and sat on one of the easy chairs abutting the wood panel.

"Did I miss something?" she asked in a raspy tone.

"Just told mama the good news – we are getting married."

"Hooked up! Great, my brother, you are the man! Wait until I tell Rosalind Allen. She won't believe it. She kind of digs you, John."

"That's great," he idly responded, glancing at Ernestine.

"Well, well, well," Brenda added, shaking her head side to side. Brenda would say anything that came to her mind, with no filter, as if she was some young child. She continued nosily, "Are you guys going to live together first?"

Mom raised her eyebrows and head imperiously, and admonished her, "Brenda, stop that. Act proper. They, I'm sure, are going to get married in the Baptist Church anyway."

"No, mother, his church, Saint Johns. It is up the hill toward La Jolla."

"La Jolla? Sounds so fancy," mom added reservedly. "I am sure our side of the family would prefer a simple, local wedding."

"We have already decided; it is a nice church. His mother will make all the arrangements with the monsignor. You can pick the choir if you wish."

"I saw it coming," Brenda interrupted. "You two love birds, shoot, you will make a fine couple and shake up this Tanner Street. Yes, a fine couple like, who was it, Diana Ross and that white guy, they had all those kids—"

"But they are divorced now," Earlene added. "Not sure what happened; maybe too much pressure from celebrities and fans, job demands… it's sad."

The couple knew what this remark, this innuendo pointed to: your life will be hard, with constant stares, glares, ostracism, and eventual defeat. They knew different.

"People get divorced and separated for various reasons," John commented defensively. "That's them. We plan on living forever." He put his arm around Ernestine, smiled, and stared into the center of the room. They sat down on the couch across from Brenda, who kept staring at them, and when caught, she would watch the western with Matt Dillon chasing some bandit.

"I remember it was not long ago, maybe three years, when you two came through the door together as a couple," mom said, deep in reminiscing, shaking her head. "It was a shock at first, but you look good together... It reminds me way back in the sixties..." Now the mother trailed off into endless memories. "When David Frost really loved Diahann Carroll, he did not want to give her up. She was a catch, and he knew it, but it didn't work out. I think it was, let me see, in 1973."

Always race, controversy, a hidden message, as the young, ebullient couple idly listened to the gossip, the rhetoric, mom Earlene's memories of days gone by never to return. She even added another celebrity couple that ended in failure. They pretended to listen, shaking their heads in derision, silent so as not to upset the mother. The new crowd, the new generation, was, in a sense, stronger, more balanced, educated, and open to new ideals and ways of bridging the gap between distrust and hatred, crossing over into peace and security. The new generation realized that life was difficult, inherently, whether you were married to someone or living together. The *status quo*, the dominant culture, the propaganda, the Leave it to Beaver generation was fading away, always attempting to push back; but the new forces, the new groups of people immigrating into the country, were setting up their own institutions, their own values. What seemed to work, over time, was this melding and meeting of people of various races in a defined space, balancing each other out, sharing individual values to create a new self, a new country, a new creation that was vital and indestructible. These couples, Black and white, Indian, and Hispanic, Asian, and Persian, had to be strong to fend off the constant stupidity, constant violence, constant attacks, of a culture that was disintegrating over time. The economy, government, and military may be strong and vibrant, but it was the individual human nature and the psyche that was constantly evolving and pushing towards new vistas and experiences.

When her mom excused herself to go finish dinner in the kitchen, John leaned over close to Ernestine's ear and asked, "Are we going to have problems with this Spencer guy? I never did like him from what you told me of him."

"Him," she huffed. "Don't worry about his sorry ass. I'll handle him if he shows up here again. He sure has some nerve. People can't let things go, and they are sorry when it is too late. He's a sad man that drinks too much and chases other women; no one wants to deal with that. He will never get married because, deep down, he doesn't want to."

"Yes, and deep down he is a player, a kid who never grew up. It's not just job and nice clothes, you must have integrity," John asserted, as Ernestine stopped and stared: she knew this was a nugget of truth.

She said, "Let's forget him. He is a part of the past I am trying to forget."

John nodded his head in assent, and dwelled on Susan Swanson, his past, now his cross to bear, this issue to resolve quickly and finally. *She is a crass individual to think she can park her car outside where I live and not say anything, and then almost run me over. Are you trying to taunt me? Why are you tracking me down after a year? This is creepy, and if I see you again, I am going to pull your hair and say 'Don't come back here ever again or I will call the police and have you arrested!'* He was seething in his mind about this; he did not expect an old college chum who was supposed to be educated, articulate, and stable to display this odd behavior. And the roommate Ron, he will not put up with endless phone calls, hang-ups, or an old Plymouth parked outside their window. There was going to be a day of reckoning.

Brenda got up, walked up to John, and whispered, "You guys are lucky. Do you have any cute, single brothers?" she asked, giggling.

"No, not really," he tersely answered, pulling his head back toward the wall.

"What!" Ernestine interrupted. "Are you serious? Go back and sit down!"

"No, just kidding," Brenda idly answered, glancing again at John.

"I know you, girl; learn your place," Ernestine demanded.

While sitting on the chair, one arm loosely over the side and one leg over the edge, Brenda moved her forefinger between the two and boldly asked, "By the way, where did you two meet? It seems such a mystery."

They already had a rehearsed story for intriguers who wanted to know the juicy details. John looked at Ernestine quickly, and Ernestine quickly at him, and she answered pleasantly, "You wouldn't believe it. I was at the bay one day having a picnic and reading a book, when this handsome guy pulls up to me on a bike. He was so friendly and dashing—"

"Please," Brenda huffed, arms folded, suspicious.

"He really was," Ernestine continued. "He started talking to me, flashing those magnificent green eyes, and he told me he was a social worker Downtown. He said I was pretty and asked for my number. The rest is history."

"Aha," Brenda said, unsure of the fairy story. "That's what happened?"

"Yes, pretty much so," John chimed in. "I knew from the first she was the one. We dated, as you know, a few years, finished school, and now is the time to tie the knot." He finished with a confident grin on his face, as Ernestine grabbed his sweaty hand.

"You two are too mushy for me," Brenda tartly said, eyebrow raised, mouth puckered. She then added, "I like a guy that is bold, forceful."

"That is your problem," the sister asserted. "You go out with these guys who only think with their pants; you will never get anywhere with them. Try to get a quality man with goals and aspirations."

"I know some quality men, sister. But I haven't found the right one. I do want to get married someday. Hey, don't rush me, I'm only twenty-four. I want to experience life first."

"What is the story of that Dwayne guy you have been dating?"

"Him?" Brenda archly replied. "He's been around and on a good Saturday night for an easy lay." Both were shocked by the remark, mouths open. Brenda continued, "I'm not sure about him. He seems to be in and out of jobs all the time and he is living in a room in this house on Fulton Street. I don't like his roommates or whoever they are. No privacy, nothing." She appeared disgusted, face withdrawn. "Speaking of guys, did I ever show you, John, the tattoo on my lower back?"

She got up, but John stuck out his hands and said, "That is okay, I will take your word for it."

Ernestine glowered at her, sitting up on the couch. "Don't be so stupid. Don't you think it is too personal to show off your flesh. What is wrong with you?"

"You are right, you are right," she answered in appeasement. She stood up, pulled out the carton and said, "Excuse me, I need a smoke." She went outside, slamming the front door. Peace at last, Ernestine concluded.

"A piece of work," he mumbled, amused, and shook his head. Ernestine, subtly, became touchy, stroking his muscular leg, up and down, bending her head by his left ear, blowing into it, and kissing his lobe. John put his arm around her defined back, squeezing it between the soft couch and her back. With a pucker, he began stroking her lower area and feeling her behind in the tight jeans. He whispered, "You look nice today." He now began to play with her flowing black hair.

Suddenly, Earlene scuttled out of the kitchen, head down. "Do you want something to drink?"

"No, we're fine," Ernestine answered, as they quickly removed the groping hands. "We plan on heading out soon, run a few errands." She stared at John intensely, then added, "We may stop over at his mom's house to pop the news."

"Oh, of course, she doesn't know yet?" her mom flatly replied. She sat down again, heavily, into the depressed green floral chair, grabbed a few pills, put them in her mouth and drank from a faded glass on the side of the table.

"John, how is work, and what do you exactly do?" she probed.

He answered, "I work in a Downtown residential program on Ash Street."

"What's that?" she asked.

"A residential program for the poor who need a place to stay. I set up case plans and help people get resources and benefits. The pay is decent, we have a small staff of fifteen workers. It's an entry level job that has room for growth. They, by the way, plan on building a large multi-million-dollar facility Downtown to house over four hundred families." He was animated in the telling. Mom listened unaffected, and Ernestine was arm in arm with him during the dialogue, idolizing him, staring directly into his moving face. She looked him up and down closely, safe, assured, and she wanted to grapple him in bed by tomorrow at her apartment, with no noise, no phone calls from annoying people, no thoughts of hospital work, in the dark, silent as a tomb, sipping wine, with soft jazz in the background as the candles were lit around the bedroom. She could never have too much of him, his love, devotion, cherished, his strong touch, his soft English gentleman's voice with perfect grammar, that bushy red mustache she loved to play with, stroking his defined chest with the curly brown hair, endless hair, receding, the shoulders defined from working out, his tallness and the way he put his chin on top of her head if he wanted assurance, in love, infatuated, and his toned arms around her sleek, shiny, black body, working his way down to lower areas. She thought about all of this in a few seconds as he continued to talk to her mother.

"Can you make a career out of what you do, social work?" Earlene asked.

He stumbled, slightly offended. "Of course. The field is booming as we are having increasing problems with poverty in this country, coupled with the recession, many more people are in need."

"Oh, I see," she answered, nodding her head.

He stopped the dialogue with her, glanced at the television, then looked over at Ernestine and patted her thigh. He, too, searched her face, as Ernestine was in idle gossip with her mother, and he had the distinct memory of when he entered the apartment after their dispute, and she was lying almost naked in red lingerie yesterday. He would never forget that moment, so sudden, so unexpected. She beckoned to him, and he was weak and willing. He treasured the moment because it was perfect, and he needed love and solace. He had this image of his queen, his Queen of Sheba, toned, and pulling him towards the couch, taking charge, determined, with her soft skin, the smell of powdered soap, her flowing hair, parted on the side like Marilyn Monroe; she was his celebrity, so glamorous, always able to say the right words, even in silence or a look. He recalled grabbing the side of her legs in their desiring not ever to let go, no fear, no inhibition, a coupling in a world that did not want them.

Brenda entered the house, "So how is work? I heard you got a job at a retail store?"

Brenda looked at him as if he was crazy. "It's okay, just a dumb job. I spend all day stacking and stocking items on shelves. You ask me, I hate it, real drudgery work. I don't plan on staying there long. I may go back to school and get a degree or something."

John stared at Brenda, and noticed she was thinner than Ernestine but had the same features, her hair in a short afro, her eyes looked deep and sleepy, if not mean, not overtly friendly, cautious, and ready to pounce if someone said or did the wrong thing. Brenda was harder than Ernestine, gruff, her behavior forced at times, even arrogant in conversation as if she knew everything. She was not only young, she was wild and immature.

"What type of degree did you want to get into? I recommend Social Services since there are so many opportunities out there, with grants and loans; it's easy."

Brenda's face said she did not believe what John just said, or she really did not care to pursue education. She stated, "It may be easy for you, but some of us must struggle to get what we want. I will keep it in mind, though." Her face and tone were apathetic, and John dropped the conversation there, and looked towards Ernestine for help.

"Brenda," Ernestine quietly pleaded, "I want you to be in my wedding as a bridesmaid. Do you want to?"

"Of course, I would not miss it for the world; you do not have to ask me that, it is a given. I need a smoke." She got up carefully, pulled out a Marlboro from the pack, and went outside.

"Honey," Ernestine said, staring at John, "ready to head out?" She patted his arm as a signal to leave. He said of course, of course, locked arms, stood up and she said, "Mom, thanks for everything. See you soon."

The mother waved at them. "Bye, you two, and congratulations again."

They left silently together, Ernestine briefly turning around, waving, her mom listless in the chair, glaring at the television. They went out the front door and Brenda was down the path, smoking easily on her cigarette. She stated as they passed, "Well, you two have a good one. John, it was so nice seeing you." She emphasized the last few words fuzzily, leering at him, sizing him up.

"Bye, Brenda, have a nice day," he responded, firmly looking ahead, arm in arm with his fiancée as they moved toward the curb and entered the car.

"What shall we do next? I am glad that is over," he said, starting the vehicle.

She put her finger to her chin, glancing out the window, into the fading light, and spoke confidently, "Let's stop by your mom's place for a short visit. I'm tired and want to go home after that."

# CHAPTER 7

"I think you should begin moving your stuff into my apartment. It will give us a chance to save some money and pay for the wedding expenses," Ernestine said, showing her practicality. "What do you think, honey?"

John was driving his blue Pontiac, attempting to concentrate, his mind racing on issues, changes, events, stupid Susan, his unsure mother, and work. He replied, looking over at her, "I think that is a good idea. I will give Ron and management my notice to move in a month. Are you sure about me moving in now?"

"I want to keep a close eye on you and make sure you don't find some other Black girl to steal you away." She said this in jest, her eyes askance at him, coy, her head leaning towards him. She knew he was loyal to the bone, yet she could not predict what sisters would do with entrapment, short skirts, tight pants hugging hips, wiggling figures, and bold brash ways to find 'a hookup'. She had to be sure, careful, and her also around the doctors and Italian Rico at work.

"Why do you think Black girls dig me?" he said.

"It is your presence and your big butt... the sisters like that; you are part of the click. They can sense when a guy likes them and wants some action. Why are you thinking about that now?"

"No reason. I was just wondering about it. I never would have thought it would happen to me, finding a nice, dark girl. I was missing out on stuff for so long, now my mind has changed. I am a part of the Black culture now; I hope that is not stupid to say."

"Stupid, stupid?" she emphasized. "It is not stupid at all. You change me a lot, too. Everyone must adjust to the person they are involved with. With you" – she paused to feebly laugh – "I first had to clean your ass up. I had to shave your neck, throw those ridiculous clothes away, and that thick, hick belt, shoot, that went straight into the trash can. You have been exposed to jazz, you have rhythm on the dance floor, your clothes match, you wear expensive cologne… you are the total man."

"And you," he answered excitedly, "I got you involved in classical literature, watching sports, and eating good Italian food, and keeping yearly traditions."

"Yes, you sure did, babe," she replied. "I respect those qualities you have, like integrity, goodness, compassion. I wish I had some of those traits." She stopped momentarily and delved further, "So, when did you know you wanted to date and be with a Black woman?"

Surprisingly, he was not offended, but calm. "I told you before, it happened a long time ago. I saw things in my family and remarks they said about Black people, and the n word was used. I was confused and angry. Years later, I became curious because I was tired of being stuck in sterile defined roles, being told what to do, what not to do. And then my mother, of all people, tried to set me up on dates with her friends' daughters, always blonde, and they were so stoical to me, not very friendly, and usually I went on one date and that was it. I believed there was more to life, more excitement, more chances, more variety. I was always attracted to dark, exotic beauties who I could relate to, who were outgoing, friendly, not trying to be secretive. Yes, girl, I love chocolate women." He said this so seriously and forcefully. He inquired, "What about you?"

"My story is a bit different. I was trapped in the only relationship I had with a Black man who was devious, a cheater, a drinker. I became so disgusted with him and living at home with my mom and all the neighbors acting like ghetto fools, no men around worth dating, nothing. I decided to take a chance. I never had prejudices against any race, and I think going to college opened new avenues for me, latest ideas that taught me to question things, and make changes in my life. I knew some white friends in school, but was too afraid to try, to reach out, to date outside of my race. Then, one day, it hit me, something came over me like a spirit, a feeling, peace. I decided to meet you and take a chance on living again."

The car sped on toward his mother's house, climbing some of the canyons to the destination.

"It should be all over the streets by now," Ernestine idly surmised.

"What is?" he asked.

"You know, those two, mom and Brenda, have already called several people and family members about the big news, going by neighbors' houses, spreading the gossip. Hear ye, hear ye, hear ye, Ernestine Jones is engaged to some white guy who looks like Tom Selleck."

"I don't know if I should be mad or honored. I wish my family would act the same way."

The word was getting out on Tanner Street, with neighbors hooting and aahing. People were asking questions. Who is he? Where did these two meet? What church for the wedding? Will they cater food and booze? What is his family like? It was as if Paul Newman and Joanne Woodward were getting married way back in the fifties and everyone was concerned with every detail. They were pushed to the forefront in the family; certain members were hoping to be invited and were already planning their outfits, their dates, the presents. Ernestine and John only hoped for a sacred day, a sacred wedding that people would remember for a long time, which would erase any doubts of their love for each other. Love knocks down barriers, mistakes, foibles. Many skeptics said to themselves that the marriage would not last, it was going to be difficult to accept, and their reputation may suffer if they were associated with or condoned the ceremony. After all, some of these people, from both sides, must stick to the clan, their racial group, their socioeconomic group, and, at the least, they were indifferent to the arrangement. They will be quiet about it and not show their disapproval in front of them and their parents; oh no, they don't want to be labelled as an agitator or racist.

The car was almost there at the condo complex near his old school; nothing had changed in the local landscape. It was late afternoon when he pulled into the carport.

"Ready? It is your turn," he said.

"Ready as I'm ever going to be. I'm confident, let's go," she asserted.

They got out of the car together, and he let her walk a little ahead of him, as he gazed at her, pretending to search for something in his car. She was stunning today, walking with that seductive gait, her hips swerving in the tight blue pants, immaculate dress shoes, her sleek arms swinging, with a silver bracelet dangling on her left wrist, and his favorite hoop earrings shining in the light. She stopped walking, turned back, annoyed. "What are you waiting for, stupid?"

"Nothing. Coming, coming," he hurriedly said as he scooted up to her, and together they walked the short distance to the door, and rang the bell, their feet shuffling in place due to anxiety.

A few seconds later, Anne Earley opened the door and smiled. "It is so good to see you, Johnnie... give me a hug." He awkwardly did so, and then she hugged Ernestine and said, "So good to see you, dear, come in."

They entered the quiet, cold condominium and sat on the red cloth couch. They kept their hands to themselves, sitting up straight like statues ready to pose for a picture. The mother had a limp now, and she grimaced as she sat down on a chair.

"Do you want something to drink? I will pour some iced tea." She did not wait for an answer, impulsively getting up and hobbling towards the kitchen, bringing out an ancient, yellow glass pitcher full of tea. She poured it at the table, sauntered over to them without a word, and handed them two large glasses. "Drink up," she commanded.

"What's your drink?" John said, knowing it was liquor.

"Oh, I am drinking a Black Russian," she answered, reaching for the tumbler at the table and taking a long draught with her head raised. Mom appeared a little tipsy.

"What brings you two to my neck of the woods?" she inquired, her voice loud and with a half-smile on her face. John studied it, wondering if mom should put down the glass so as not to be irascible.

"Where's Danny?" he deflected.

"Gone. Terrible. He has been missing since this morning. He returns late at night," Anne answered, shaking her head, play acting for sympathy.

"What is he doing for himself that is productive?" he sullenly queried.

"He works. He says he does sales of some sort... He did graduate from college, and I give him credit for that." Mom trailed off her words with a look of despair, head down momentarily, her face processing inner, destructive thoughts. She continued, "Let's not worry about him. What are you two up to?"

Ernestine, forcing manners and animation, inserted, "Work, work all the time. We may go to see a movie later, honey; what do you think?"

"Maybe." He was poked to say what he said. He did not like fake behavior and saying things he did not want to say and feel; he had too much of this growing up in a setting where secrets were kept, feelings avoided or not validated, snooping antics of the mother trying to find out all her kids' innermost thoughts, trying to mold them to her world view, her Catholicism, steering them away from their father, of whom she had a seething resentment. He stared directly ahead at his mother in the chair sitting up, knees held together in the flowing skirt, and he placidly uttered, "Mom, Ernestine and I have decided to get married. We just got engaged." He rubbed Ernestine's back.

Mom, with no effect on her face for a few seconds, answered with a smile that seemed painful, "That is marvelous! I'm so happy for you two… You will be married in the Catholic Church, right?"

"Of course we are; where else?" he responded. "We hope you can set it up with the monsignor for us when we set a date."

"Sure, sure, I would be glad to. Don't forget that you must go to the engagement encounter first before the service, that's required." He did not answer and waved his hand.

"You sure got a good son here," Ernestine pleasantly added, patting his back. "I'm lucky to have found this diamond in the rough." She stated this assuredly, trying to placate any misgivings about the announcement. Ernestine and John believed mom was, now, genuinely happy, but were not totally convinced because of her demeanor and past remarks and silence when any subject regarding personal relationships was concerned; and that dirty word about sex or living together was never broached; it was taboo, and mom never thought about it any more, hidden and depleted. If

Anne believed that they should have been married a long time ago, she was sadly mistaken, because the couple wanted John to graduate, get settled, and then begin a career. They were patient in the waiting, the development of their connection, their love, and the time passed quickly, until the day at the beach, at the perfect moment, at peace, an urging to commit themselves was spoken as if it was preordained at the instant, on that June day in 1982, with the beach and waves rolling in the background and the wind touching their faces.

"We have your blessing, mom?" he continued, straining forward, hoping for the right reply.

"Of course, darling. Let me know if you folks need any help with anything. Who is the best man?"

"Probably Brad."

"Oh, sure, he is such a good, loyal friend. What about Danny in the wedding party?"

"Not sure about that," he replied with annoyance. "Danny has been away in the Navy for the last couple of years. I don't see him much, and he doesn't seem too supportive these days."

There was an awkward pause, a dreadful silence due to the troublesome younger brother, with his occasional outbursts that annoyed and offended John and Ernestine when they came over. This mysterious and fiery sibling had only been seen by her a few times: either he refused to come out of his room, or he was gone on some romp, some adventure to make a million dollars. Ernestine could not decide on what type of person he truly was due to his presenting himself with false airs and bravado that he was better than anyone else. Then, on other days and occasions, he would laugh and carry on deep conversations with you on the economy, the country, literature, his favorite hobby – chess – and the strategies involved with it, and his favorite sport – baseball – with commentary of teams and stats.

"Well, you decide what to do," his mom idly replied. "I can't make the decision for you, but—"

"We will talk it over, Anne, and let you know," Ernestine quickly added. "We will see if he even wants to be in the wedding. He is shy and may not want to."

Anne Earley shook her head, docile, dwelling on her old marriage, failed, insipid, too many years of fighting over bills, and John's father, Joseph: too many lost jobs, firings, quitting. The warfare ended in disaster and divorce in October 1979. Anne could not bring energy or peace to the present moment of her son's happy announcement. She forced a smile, got up and went to the kitchen and barked out, "Do you guys want something to eat? I have spaghetti and meatballs just like mom used to make." She was referring to her Italian mother, Maria Vicelli, who was married to an Englishman and came over on the boat in the New York area in the early nineteen hundreds. From what John remembered, they were happy at the house when his family visited, although his mother, over time, painted or hinted at trouble in the marriage, and Anne resented her mother for some queer reason. John and Ernestine concluded it was due to her olive, dark complexion that Anne refused to validate and accept.

"Honey, do you want to stay?" John asked with a squeaky voice.

Ernestine was nervous, unsure. "Why sure, if it is not too much trouble, Anne," she cried out, calling her by the first name and afraid to call her 'mom' for the present moment.

"No trouble, just sit down, I'll call you. It will be nice."

Anne was heard banging some dishes, silverware, setting the table feverishly like a busy beaver, moving, sipping another Black Russian, the television console blaring some archaic movie from the fifties in black and white. If you saw this house, you would believe it resembled a museum of trinkets and treasures. Knick-knacks and ceramics were placed everywhere in two large cabinets, lined up perfectly, new, with no chips; a row of books in a bookcase, impressive, to include Trollope, Dumas, Twain, Tolstoy, Cather, several biographies, Anne Morrow Lindbergh books, all these tomes pristine in dustjackets; another shelf had numerous paperbacks, mostly classic and romantic novels lined up in perfect rows. She was proud of the collection, and would encourage John to borrow several books, which he never did. An odd Spanish fireplace that the father once hated, had been in the family since the sixties, was mounted to the wall, and had two cabinets that opened out, and inside were liquor bottles and a few statues. The dining room consisted of a cherished, expensive Spanish-style table with six chairs, and Anne would use some type of oil to keep the wood shiny. On the ground floor was a small bathroom, and around the living room were several oil painting prints of Degas and Manet in wooden frames. The upstairs included a master and two smaller bedrooms, with the beds made with pressed sheets and blankets denoting no visitors were allowed there for secret affairs. The younger son's room was a mess, with clothes scattered everywhere on the floor, books piled up on a desk, and a small Emerson television was mounted on top of a faded brown dresser. Outside, the old condominium complex was the same as when John had lived there for years while in college: empty, narrow lanes, and neighbors you never saw or knew. It was clean, the streets newly paved, and children were not allowed to play in the streets and were relegated to a small park located in the middle of this large complex.

"You know, John, I will be moving out of here soon. I can't afford the rent on my salary any more," his mother said, defeated.

"Where will you go?" Ernestine asked, concerned.

"There is a two-bedroom senior complex up the hill. I've applied there and I'm just waiting for a vacancy."

"Is Danny going, too?" John harshly asked, his arms folded.

"Of course, until he gets on his feet. I can't get rid of my son."

John huffed, shaking his head, then looked at Ernestine for a reaction. There was none.

Dinner was served in a few minutes; the steaming pasta and bread could be smelled from the couch where they sat. John escorted Ernestine by the arm and pulled out the seat for her and sat down, fingering their napkins in place. They were hungry, their eyes scanning the tabletop, the spaghetti and meatballs piled high on a large plate, a Caesar salad fluffed in a wooden bowl, and French bread, hot, was sliced on a large plate, while three glasses of red wine were poured into green goblets – the brand was some cheap Carlo Rossi that Anne liked – and Italian salad dressing rounded out the feast.

"Gosh, this looks delicious," Ernestine politely said. "John, on occasion, makes a good spaghetti, too. He must have inherited the recipe from you."

The mom shook her head in assent. "I hope you like it; it is one of John's favorites, along with lasagna... Dig in," she urged, pointing her finger.

They were silent for a few minutes, twirling the pasta and digging into the generous salad. Ernestine knew to be proper, because her words and moves were going to be scrutinized by the mother. She ate delicately, small bites, mouth closed, one leg crossed on top of the other, eyes down, posture upright. Pass the bread, please: such good etiquette. Her mom, if nothing else, taught her to have good table manners and refined speech when in public, and to dress the part with the best clothing. John noticed this, so prim, so proper, staring, she's got to win over mother, he asserted. Who could find a better mate? She was educated, assured, wore designer clothing, had a good paying job as a nurse, owned a nice sporty white Mustang hatchback with a blue stripe down the side; her apartment was so cool, chic, clean, modern, with a wine rack, built-in bookshelves, scrubbed kitchen countertops, no trash anywhere, the house scented, modern furniture, a plush brown couch with a cover, and her jewelry somewhat expensive, with silver bracelets, ruby rings, a pricy Cartier watch – a gift from the father – her hair maintained every three weeks, the clothing cleaned, pressed, matching always with comfortable sweaters worn around the neck, and occasional scarfs like Sophia Loren, her idol, would wear, the makeup bought at Robinsons, red ruby lipstick always visible, fresh, brown powder, eyelashes noticeable, eyebrows trimmed, and Ernestine had several thousand dollars in the bank. To him, she could do nothing wrong.

Today, at the table, he really admired her, her courage, her fortitude, her life, her pushing the boundaries, her reaching out in conversation with his mother, the topic, now on the two of them going to a shopping mall in Tijuana to find some cheap frames and clothing. It was Ernestine's flair, her ability to adapt to any situation, her goodness and friendliness he found refreshing. He decided he would remember this day for a long time.

"When events are settled and you have time, dear, give me a call and we will make a day of it," Anne animatedly said, looking fondly at Ernestine. Presently, deep down, the mother saw qualities in her she deeply admired.

"Anne, I will. John won't mind, will you?" She stared at his serious face.

"No, you two have fun. Bring me a bottle of Tequila or a brown belt," he hinted. He now drank a beer he had got from the fridge, guzzled it, head down, looking at the suds in the glass, and continued, "You know, mom, she really cleaned up my act, she cut my hair, bought me some nice dressy clothes, and this Timex watch when I started the new job." He held out his right arm, childishly showing it off.

"It's nice," she tersely responded, chewing her food, scraping the plate.

"Don't be so vain," Ernestine interjected.

Surprised, he replied, eyebrow raised, "Who, me? I'm the humblest guy around. Just showing off the nice gift you got me." He eyed it and continued to pile pasta in his mouth.

"Slow down," she admonished. "And don't slurp." She scanned over to the mother as she said this, smiling. He kept on delving into the meal, grabbing a third piece of bread, intense in the eating, surveying the plates, sipping again the beer, ignoring Ernestine's command to slow down. His mother just stared, her head also lowered, chewing softy. Her face had a slight grin, her eyes sleepy and red from the liquor.

"What do you want for your birthday? It is only a few days away," his mother asked.

"Hell, I'll be twenty-four," he declared, sitting up, chest out, gulping his drink. "The big two-four. For a present, not sure, how about a Mercedes?" he smiled.

"Sure, Mercedes, with the recession and gas shortage, you want a Mercedes... How about a sweater?"

He pondered. "No, thanks; she got me a nice one a few months ago from Macy's – a brown turtleneck. No, you decide."

"You can always use another one; can't have enough sweaters," Ernestine nervously asserted, head down, hoping his mother was not upset or offended for turning down the gift.

Mom stared at Ernestine, shaking her head. "He is always hard to please. That's his nature: picky!"

He received a kick from his fiancée, and then shortly later said, "I guess a sweater will do." He stared at her, perked up and stated, "I got taste now. I read *GQ* magazine. She turned me on to it, and the styles in there are just what I need. Style is important, you know. That's what happens when you settle down and meet the right woman." He patted Ernestine's lap and gave her a fond smile.

Switching, Ernestine put down her fork. "Well, Anne, what is new with you? Your house looks tremendous with all of these ceramics and souvenirs. It must have taken you years to collect them."

"Bargains. I got them mostly at bargain centers, some at some garage sales. I hardly ever pay over ten dollars for anything. You see that pug dog over there?" – pointing to a cabinet – "Eight dollars; such a deal!" she gloated in the telling of this to impress her.

"I see," Ernestine quietly replied, turning her head around to view the cabinet shelf. "I wouldn't mind owning one of them myself," she added brightly.

"Your father," Anne said with a smirk, glaring at the son, "he never would buy me anything. I had to do it on my own."

They were shocked that she had brought up, resurrected, the dead past, and mom chewed slowly on her food, head down, face sour, angry, seething, now caught in her past, always resurfacing, because it was never resolved or forgotten. For a moment, John remembered vaguely the trip they took to Montauk Point one summer long ago, but mother was so angry that his father had impulsively bought a camera, against the tight budget, stating he needed it, and it was talked about for years, when they were fighting or buying something for the house, the stupid camera incident, much bigger than it was; it was the person that Anne hated more.

"I guess so. Dad was more into books than trinkets," John concluded.

"Books! Books! That was all he did was to read those stupid books! If he had spent more time in the office or finding a solid job, things would have been better. Anyway, let's change the subject." She finally stopped, trying to compose herself, her demeanor attempting to shift to happiness.

Ernestine was shocked, unsure of what to say or do. She knew these issues because her family had them, too: her father hated, hidden, a philanderer, and her mother would never forgive him for these faults. John stared at Ernestine and was embarrassed at the tirade, his family past putting its mark on the present dinner.

John said, "Mom, that's okay. Forget it." His voice trailed off as he finished his dinner, while his mom scraped her plate, and his girlfriend put her hand on his lap in a form of condolence.

"Now that you two are getting married," Anne continued, "what plans do you have for living arrangements? It might be better, John, if you moved in and give you a chance to save some money."

They were both stunned that his dear old Catholic mother would even say this. It made sense to them and that was their plan, but for Anne to assert this was unusual, and John viewed her in a different light as someone who was progressive and liberal. He knew mom did go out on a few dates with an older, wealthy gentleman, but he was not sure, nor did he want to know, what went on behind closed doors. His mother told him, once, recently, that this man, Bill, was a gentleman, and she hinted that there was a budding relationship, a chance at happiness, and his mother, for all her faults, seemed to be alive again when she mentioned his name. Mom constantly put on this appearance of celibacy, unhappiness, no attachment to men, but occasionally the old flame came back.

"You two are so lucky," mom said. "If only Danny could settle down and find a nice girl."

They at first didn't know what to say, but John commented, "When he was in the service, didn't he know some Asian woman he had been dating? He told me he was crazy about her, and she would write him all the time."

Anne Earley had an immediate, sour expression. "Never met her. I don't know if she was real or made up. I tried to set him up on a few dates with Joan's daughter – you remember them – but he wouldn't do it. Stubborn."

Anne was so funny to Ernestine in her simplistic, bombastic way. She would at one moment appear so pleasant, affectionate, and the next instance, it was like some demon possessed her to change her whole personality. Ernestine knew that John's past family life and struggles were mild compared to all the violence she had to endure in the ghetto, within her own family, and her mother even had a large butcher knife under her bed to threaten Jerry Jones to change his sinful ways or to ward off intruders who came to the door to cause a ruckus. It was the hidden, repressed twenty-year marriage of Anne and Joseph Earley that defined who they were and were to be: unchanged attitudes, unchanged behavior, unresolved pain, from these two who were born in the Great Depression and a culture that was now obsolete to the new generation.

John wanted to tell his mother to quit being so nosy and intrusive, to mind her business and not to fix anyone up on stupid, orchestrated dates where everyone had to put on a front, with no connection or passion with some young girl who didn't know what they wanted except to be pretty and pampered.

"I think the best thing for Danny boy is to work, keep working, save money in the bank, and find his own place. Everyone will be happier. He is twenty-two now, and you could help him locate a shared apartment."

"It is easier said than done," his mother replied, perturbed. "He is like a gypsy around here and I don't know what he does with his money. He says he is buying books on economics and business and wants to invest. Frankly, I think that's dumb and a waste of time."

"He's got to grow up some time, and you need to stop coddling him," John added, putting down his fork on the empty plate and sitting back.

Ernestine broke the tension. "I sure molded you. You were like your brother: young, inexperienced. You didn't know what you wanted… It takes time to find out who you are. I am sure he will figure it all out."

"You met him several times; what do you really think? He seemed to be always the center of attention as if no one else existed."

"Like I said, he is young and a little rough around the edges, sort of like my sister, Brenda. It's all growing pains," she diplomatically asserted, staring at Anne, who sat there in sour silence, with her hands together, and elbows on the table.

Anne Earley, reserved, chimed in, "This is getting nowhere, honey. How is the nursing job?"

"Glad you asked. I've been there six years, pay is good, great benefits, and good news… I told you, honey; I am up for a promotion for head nurse in my department."

"Head nurse, that's great. But are you going to have a problem?" Anne asked, face forward on the table.

"Problem? What problem do you mean?" she replied, confused, shaking her head.

"Not with rude men making advances. I mean, with the promotion upsetting some of the staff who are narrow minded, not wishing some Black person to succeed over them."

"Not sure if that's a problem. I work hard, am popular, why wouldn't I be considered for the position?"

There was a tense pause, a look, mom red-faced from all the drinks consumed, her light brown hair disheveled. "I don't have a problem with it, but other folks just don't seem to accept the changing ways, you know."

"Mom," John interrupted, "that's stupid, a dumb remark, and I'm surprised you said it. Why did you ever bring it up? She can have any job she wants and get it without these hang-ups."

"I wasn't implying anything negative; we know she is qualified and should have the charge nurse position. I don't know; in my day, not long ago, they were really choosy on who they wanted or did not want. I am all for you, honey; you get that job! And don't let anyone step over you." Anne's message was cryptic, as she picked up the remaining Black Russian, the ice melted, stirred it, and drained off the remainder with a big gulp, looking straight ahead, trying to force a pleasant disposition. It was not working, as the atmosphere was strained.

John broke the silence. "Mom, you had jobs where you were promoted, right?"

"Yes, several," she replied quietly.

"So, what is the message here? Why wouldn't Ernestine be promoted? I hope skin tone does not have anything to do with it."

"Of course not, why should it? We are in different times now where that does not really matter any more. Let's forget the whole thing," Mom added, a little embarrassed.

Ernestine was reserved, and finally said, "It will all work out. I should have an answer after I am interviewed next week. I am a shoo-in for the job."

John rose from the table, threw the napkin carelessly down over his plate, and pulled on Ernestine's arm. "Let's go and sit over there on the couch. Are you done eating?"

"Yes," she happily answered. "Thank you, Anne, for the dinner. It was great."

"Glad you guys liked it. Do you want some cake?"

"Maybe later," Ernestine placated, as John led her to the living room to watch an inane show on the large color console.

Under his breath, his face close to hers, he said, "We should be taking off in a few minutes. I apologize for my mom's rude behavior."

Fortunately, his mother got up to place the dirty dishes in the sink around the corner, out of earshot.

"She just had a few too many drinks. It's comical, and I didn't take much offense to it," Ernestine said.

"I did!" he asserted, pointing a finger down at the couch. He slumped backwards, looking at the table, mom washing dishes. "I tell you, I am a bit embarrassed by the whole thing, the innuendos; maybe it's nothing, but it sure didn't come out right."

Anne came into the living room, calm, formal, placid. "Come in and have some cake," she insisted.

"We have to take off, and we had so much to eat," Ernestine said. "Maybe next time."

Anne stared, her head shaking nervously side to side; then she sighed, and moved back to the kitchen. John had noticed the shaking over the last few years, and wasn't sure what it was; perhaps a medical condition that needed attention. It was just another odd mannerism of his mother that he could not explain or repair; his mother was who she was, and you could not really change anything about her because she was too stubbornly entrenched in neurosis and silly antics.

The room was silent as mom continued to bang and wash plates in the kitchen. "Are you guys okay?" she yelled.

"Yes, Mom, never better," he answered, staring at Ernestine, his eyes closed, trying to dispel some of the table conversations that were building up resentment in him; the same issues, the wandering brother, the hidden remarks from his mother, made him an unwanted stranger at home. "Come on, honey," John urged. "Grab your purse, quick."

They moved slowly to the door, and Ernestine added, "Thanks again for the dinner; it was great. I will call you about the shopping date."

Mom came out of the dim-lighted kitchen, stepped toward the door, and received a weak hug from both. They waved and went out into the street toward the car. Now free, breathing fresh air, Ernestine pondered and said, "Your mom is a strange one. Sometimes I can't quite figure out her coldness. Maybe she means well."

"Me neither," he said in support. "Let's head back. I will drop you at home and call you tomorrow."

# CHAPTER 8

Early, around six in the morning, John's telephone rang. He was startled out of his bed as it kept ringing, it seemed, at a deafening volume. In the dark, he got up, put his fingers over his eyes to rub out the sleep, and ran to the living room. Picking up the receiver, he said, "Hello, hello."

A soft, barely audible voice answered, "John, this is Susan."

His eyes wandered and his heart began to pound. "Sue, it's early, six a.m. What is the trouble?"

"Trouble? No trouble. I wanted to check in because I miss you. You never call me."

"Why? What for? What's this all about? Has something happened?"

"No. Can you do me a favor? Can you meet me on campus by the Revelle Library under the tree, say around nine o'clock?"

"Why there…? Can't this wait?"

"No, it's important, and I thought that is a safe place so no one would know our business. I would like to see you before I go."

"Go? Where are you going? Back home to the folks?"

"I'll explain it then. See you soon."

She hung up the phone, and John stared at the receiver held tightly in his hand, tight, before putting it down gently and glancing at his roommate's door. No one stirred. He heard the ticking of the clock. He rubbed his eyes and face and could not believe that Susan had called and sounded so desperate, so vague. Should he go to the meeting on campus? He initially ignored it, but concluded that it would be best to close the doors, forever, on this past relationship, to clear his mind of any guilt, to say goodbye to this student and keep the Three Musketeers in the past, dead, buried where it belonged. If he did not go, then Susan Swanson would just continue harassing him, and he could not exist in that situation.

John made some coffee, got dressed, and watched the clock for two hours until it was time to leave. He called in sick for work and his calendar was free.

He struggled to call Anna Cohen, his other school friend, who was close to Susan, but she may not care if Susan lived or died; she was moving on to her own career and the best thing was to leave behind this senseless episode. College life was indeed gone, to be remembered, but never to replace the present, mature aspirations. It could never be recaptured since it was a rite of passage for most who struggled onward with life, love, and work.

He drove out to the UCSD campus and parked his car across Torrey Pines Road, locked it, stretched, and stared at the rising sun. Donning his sunglasses, he headed to one block, entering the south side of the campus filled with pine and eucalyptus trees, the same ones as when he was a young student at seventeen, on his first day of class, lost in the abyss of foliage and buildings.

He drew closer to the famous large tree beside the gray library structure he had spent hours under to discuss ideas, read or eat lunch. Many of these days here were with Anna, and some with Susan, depending on the class schedule. They studied, reflected, laughed, and pushed themselves to find knowledge and wisdom, dreaming of a happy future with solid careers to show for their efforts. Nothing would stop them in their indestructible youth and fervor, and they believed they knew everything. Moving with conviction, he saw Susan, wearing brown pants and a yellow shirt, standing under the tree; she idly waved, then crossed her arms, and her hair was neatly parted in the middle.

John approached to within a few yards of her. She stood erect, glaring at him as he came close enough to be heard. She did not offer to hug him, nor did he presently want to. "John, so good to see you," she said with a smile and wrinkles in the corner of her squinting eyes.

He paused, faked a smile. "What is it, Sue? You sounded so desperate."

"Desperate? I would not use that word," she responded in a lecturing, volatile tone. "You know what is wrong, what you did."

He shook his head in derision. "What are you talking about? I haven't had any contact with you in about a year, until you decided to call my house, hang up on me, and then you have the audacity to park your car in my lot, and when I went outside to find out what was going on, you almost ran me over! Explain that!"

"John, darling, nothing to explain. I want to ask you a deep question." She had a smirk on her face, her arms folded, arrogant, her eyes piercing. "Who is this chick you are dating?"

Instantly, he replied, "It's none of your business. I told you about her a few years back at school. Why do you want to know?"

She paused, calmly staring straight at him, her finger pointed. "I don't think she is the right one for you, is all."

"Not the right one? Well, who is?" he responded, trying to force the issue to the surface.

"Me," she answered with a serious face, now moving towards him a few feet away. "It's always been me, hasn't it? We shared good times, and honestly, I am surprised you haven't called me. Anna calls me, why not you?" She stopped a moment and brashly added, "Guys like me, and have tasted my fruits."

He inhaled deeply, shocked, sensing Susan's nervous behavior, arms trembling, moving, her motions jerky, her talk bold. "Susan, I don't call you because you are not my girlfriend. It is time to move on, and quite frankly, I do not know why you called me out to this place."

"Remember, this was the tree where we three met." She pulled out a snapshot from her small purse. John jumped, because he would not put it past her if she had a knife or weapon. She handed him a small snapshot photo of John,

Anna, and herself smiling under this tree, in sophomore year. "You do remember this?" she repeated for effect.

He took the three by five photo from her quickly, looked at it, handed it back, and uttered, "So what. It is a nice photo; you keep it."

She looked at him now fondly, starting to archly smile, and continued, her words slurring, "This is us as it should be, me and you, together. I haven't forgotten the last date we had, and why you did not pursue me. Why, why? John, don't you like me?"

He was alarmed and felt pity for her in her crass delusion. "Susan, it's over, that's that. Move on and don't call me any more."

"I'll do whatever I want, honey. You should change your mind and drop that black chick. She's not the one for you… I am." She tried to touch his arm, but he removed it quickly, stepping back. "Really, why be so shy?" she beckoned.

"Are you smoking something? I think you are smoking some funny stuff. I haven't seen this side of you before. You used to be a good student, a good person; now, I don't know who you are," he ended nervously, unsure of what Susan would say or do. She may make a scene on campus and the police may be called, or she might just walk away and then continue to call and harass him. He believed it would not end until she relocated, or he changed his number. The campus was quiet, with only a few students walking on the sidewalks.

"If I could help you, I would, but I can't solve this… problem," he said.

"There is no one else but you, you know it, you are trying to avoid it. I sensed you wanted me when I kissed you. Come, don't act stupid. Really, I will make you happy." She said this nervously, laughing, her mouth open in a surly way, and her whole demeanor and body was intensified and agitated.

"Bye, Sue, I am leaving. Don't follow me." John turned and left her there near the pepper tree, turning around in case she attacked him.

She was alone, spurting out senseless words of love and endearment. "Please come back! Come back! I hope I haven't offended you! Call me!" she barked out.

He kept walking, with his head to the side, as she yelled, "You dumb son of a bitch!"

He continued his gait as he waved his arm in disgust behind him and exited the campus. He located his car on the street, and looked back to see if she was following him. Sorry Susan was not there, and he exhaled. Now, he concluded, he would have to change his number. She may come back again to his apartment any time she wished. Is she crazy? What is the obsession? Why me? Do I tell Ernestine the details of this meeting? He decided that she would not understand fully the import of it all and it would hamper his connection to her. She will always think that there was the possibility of a relationship on the side, and she was the jealous type. She had been damaged already with her old boyfriend, Spencer, and would never let it happen again.

He drove in a trance back east on the highway to his apartment. It was near nine thirty in the morning and Ron would be gone to work. He arrived at the complex, scurried up the stairs, went in, deadbolted the door, and his back was against it in contemplation. He took a deep breath and went to the kitchen window. No gold Plymouth Duster was to be seen.

He sat languidly on the couch, tired, eyes half shut, concerned with Susan in his thoughts. He debated calling Anna, but decided not to worry her on this intense conundrum. "Leave it alone," he said. "Susan will just forget all about it in her mania and find a new target." He did not realize what had transpired. Susan and John were innocent friends with no pretensions, just immature students with no motives with each other; he was not sexually attracted to her, and no impression that he would ever pursue her. They, he said in validation, were only study partners and that was that, and it was and ever will be just that status. *I hope she goes home to her parents' house so they can take care of her*, he mused. There is something wrong, anyone could see that, some type of illness that was taking over her body; and the drugs, whatever they are, intensifying her mood and compulsions. John knew this was the strangest thing he had to deal with outside of his brother, Danny, who was also acting out in delusions. It was one thing to be in social work and deal with all types of folks with illnesses and addictions, but when it came close to home, your life, it was very personal, real, and tiresome.

He jumped off the couch, pulled a soda out of the refrigerator, and drank it in the kitchen, attempting to get solace from the light streaming through the window. He went back to the couch, turned on a movie, and drifted off to sleep.

A few minutes later, the phone rang, and he jumped. It rang three times as he stared at it from the couch. He did not want to get it; it kept on ringing seven or eight times more, making him annoyed. He ran to the phone and said hello, but he heard only a dead space, then a click. He slammed the phone into its casing, and said, "Damn that woman! That crazy, stupid ass!"

What was he to do? He impulsively decided not to be a victim of his passions and he would drive to Coronado State Beach and sit on the sand to gather some semblance of peace. Peace, peace, he thought, a strong, good word and feeling that even this young man craved as important and crucial, for without it he would descend into destruction and despair. Quickly, he donned a baseball cap, grabbed a water bottle, snatched his keys from the dresser, picked out a sweater, and ran down the stairs to his car. He cursed under his breath, frustrated with his life presently, but resolved to find a solution to it all. In his expression, another female tenant was alarmed at his mood and words, and stared at him as if he was disturbed, and she became frightened and scurried away from him. He did not care about her attitude or judgement. He thought about Ernestine, and her goodness, and his desire to protect her from this insane episode, this sinister, brash act by Susan, and he would call the police if he needed to without fear or guilt. He did not care what happened to Susan.

Harassment, anger, anxiety were words that entered his head as he drove onto the highway to head south over the Coronado Bridge with its expansive view. A short time later he made a sharp left turn on Orange Avenue, his spirit improving as he neared the beach. On this ritzy street were various stores, antique shops, an extensive green park area with huge shaded trees, on old library that looked like a tomb, and on each side of the avenue were expensive red stucco houses and apartments recessed from the street with fancy cars in the driveway. On the right as he passed was on old, historic movie theater; moms with kids were seen in strollers crossing the intersection, cars going the opposite way to the city to work or conduct business. Then he fondly passed a burger joint on the left, famous for making huge, season burgers and he and Ernestine would go there on occasion. Further on, near the hotel, were several Mexican restaurants, a few sleepy, dark bars, and several tourist traps.

He finally made it to the Hotel Del Coronado, glancing up at its large structure, like a giant, built in 1888. It had housed famous people over the years, including Marilyn Monroe in one of her later films, and it was said to be haunted by someone who committed suicide there decades ago. He almost subconsciously swerved the small car in and out of traffic, distracted, and he found a side street, turned left, and drove down a hill to find free parking abutting several large homes.

He walked a few blocks in the rising heat of this late June morning, crossing at the light, the immense monster hotel in front of him with its red roof and white sides. He scooted down a path on the north side, past a cabana that served tacos and mixed drinks. He saw a young white girl in a skimpy bathing suit, with her nakedness for all the world to see, talking to a few older gentlemen seated on barstools. He passed by her and smiled to himself. Several other couples were at the adjoining pool area sunbathing as he headed on the sidewalk that led to the brilliant tan sand and the one hundred yards to the edge of the water. To the distant right, on a hill, was the famous Cabrillo Monument, the point where the Spanish explorer Juan Cabrillo landed centuries ago. He sat down on a bench, the breeze flowing in his face, and contemplated. Where was he now? Where was his life before? Were things better now? These qualms were testing the balance of the past with the hope of the future. John Earley, the dreamer, the thinker, was searching for an understanding of his place in the universe, and what direction his life was now taking him. The old student days were long gone, and now his fiancée, Ernestine, was beckoning him, calling and waving him to cross the divide into a new life, forever changed, so final, and so peaceful.

At the beach, this fateful day, John recalled their first meeting. It seemed ages ago, but was still fervent in his memory: in October 1979, Ernestine Jones, in blue flair jeans, a white shirt, belt-buckled shoes, silver hoop earrings, with a strong perfume, picked up John, then twenty, at a movie theater Downtown; she made the connection, the advances, as she sidled up to his seat, attracted to this handsome young man. He recalled being totally entranced with this Black siren woman: her confidence, her coyness, her charm, her impeccable looks and figure that drew John irresistibly and unavoidably to her embrace. They left the theater and got a cheap hotel room at the Golden West, with its purple façade and clock out front on the overhang. They went to a small room on the third floor, he fondly remembered. *Gosh, I was nervous*, he said to himself. He disrobed, and she, like a cat, slid across that bed and nuzzled his neck, dragging him into the center of the mattress.

She said, "Make love to me, now," in a whisper.

He recalled, fondly, her trim, sleek, dark figure, her defined breasts, her smooth skin and ample behind that he grabbed in his lust, in his love of the woman who would change his life forever. After it was over, he did not feel ashamed, although later he would go to confession to be absolved of the sin. He did not tell his mother or anyone of the rendezvous; it was his secret, his rite of passage, and his destiny; all that had gone on before, the questioning of people who used the n word, or were racist, his love of everyone who was the underdog, the minorities he gravitated towards, because in them, he saw a little of himself. She wrote down her number after the hotel romp on a small piece of paper, in flowing blue ink, which he keeps in his wallet.

He called her a few days after this tryst, pleading for a connection, aroused and mystified by this woman. They began dating, Ernestine dropping her present boyfriend, Spencer, and they decided to be loyal to each other, through thick and thin, progress or failure, resentment or acceptance, for three years until he graduated from college. For John, memory and history were important, vital, a teacher that gave one knowledge to be used forward, to learn from its lessons, and to strive for a new level of existence. He mulled over this, now, at the Coronado Beach, and decided that nothing could separate this unlikely couple, their love: not time, or people, or antiquated institutions.

He sat at that beach, under an umbrella, for almost two hours, eating a taco and having a few Coors beers. He was soon to be twenty-four; is that too early to tie the knot? His father was not much older than him when he married in the fifties at twenty-six. He believed that he was better off and more equipped from his mother and father who were, too, virgins when they met at a Brooklyn dance in 1957, so formal, so frumpy, sheltered, with no knowledge of sex or gender, only knowledge of school, Latin, Greek studies; their parents repressed, not telling them anything about life and the world, to fend for themselves. They did not know, did not care, enveloped in their own issues of shame, neuroses, fears, anxieties, and oppressions. John realized that the world of 1982 was coming into its own, with new venues, new chances, new relationships that once were forbidden, and now slowly accepted. He would not fear a slap in the face, the force of violence as in the sixties and the Civil Rights Movement; he refused to accept ridicule from anyone, not his mom, or best friend Brad, or his baseball teammates. He would forge ahead to define his own path, and if someone did not like his choice and lifestyle, he would shun them like a plague. Ernestine, he knew, felt the same way; she would not stand for crass, fake people, family members, or friends, who were hypocrites, and she dissociated from several school mates who did not approve of her choice and her mate. White was not right in their minds, and nothing she could do would deter them from this entrenched prejudice. She either tore their phone number up or told them never to call again. One did not test Ernestine Jones; she was defiant, proper, and said what was on her mind, and people misjudged her because she had a soft, easy personality. She hated the ghetto life, as she called it, where the mentality, the culture was filled with people going nowhere, comfortable with things as they are or what their parents adhered to; their life was filled with endless poverty, ignorance, rampant addiction, jail, failed marriages, babies out of wedlock, high unemployment rates, hatred, all the things that Ernestine detested in her soul.

They were patient, day in and day out, each month passing with progress, Miss Jones saving her nurse pay in a separate account, knowing John would be faithful and not date anyone else; he needed to stay the course so the relationship flowered in intensity, trust, defying logic, defying the odds and scoffers.

Now, in June 1982, he proposed boldly at a beach, barely conscious of what he said, but meaning every word. He would not fear or falter one inch, he testified.

Out of his reverie, he left the Coronado Beach, at ease, a slight buzz from the beers he had consumed, and headed back to his car. He traveled past the cabana, and, on his right, reclining in a chair, was a full-figured young Black woman, who had her hands over her eyes, staring at him in approval as he walked by. She had coffee-colored skin, a short afro, and red toenails. She wiggled in her seat so he could get a better look, interested, her lips pursed, a cocktail on the table next to her. She had on dark sunglasses, and one leg was raised and bent in a seductive pose. She continued to stare as

John stopped and sat at a table some distance from her, perplexed. The woman looked ahead, pretending not to care; she then got up to rub some lotion on her legs and back, facing away from him, giving him a nice show. She was indeed attractive, around twenty-five, slim, with short, cropped hair and toned legs. She sat down again in the chair, sipping her drink and adjusting her bathing suit. No one was in the vacant chair next to her, no boyfriend, no husband, no admirer. John fingered his mustache in his excitement and nervousness, hoping she would not see him stare at her. He looked ahead at the beach and ocean in the distance, but would glance, askance, to see what the bathing beauty was doing. The sexy, tanned girl just sat, looking idly ahead, calm, and drank from the glass. She suddenly, slowly, turned over and lay on her stomach, looking to the side, her firm behind prominent. It seemed no one else noticed her. She was gorgeous, elegant, but no man gave her a second thought. He was almost hoping a husband would come by any minute to get her, or she would go back to her hotel room. No one came. She was, to John, out of place in this exclusive hotel catering to rich white folks, and he surmised she had money to spend.

After a few minutes, John got up from his chair and left the girl there as she had her head on her side, hands underneath, her eyes following him as he left the pool area. John believed she lay there to pick up some guy to have a few drinks and then go back to her hotel room for an affair. He did not glance back. He shook off his urges and knew the girl would have been an easy pickup.

"Temptations, temptations," he flatly said. "Now that I am engaged, I seem to have more temptations than ever." He wondered about this as he walked briskly to his car, believing it was jitters of his pending marriage, or it was him, his weakness, as there will always be someone of the opposite sex there, available, to be a stumbling block or just a fantasy. Nothing had changed, really, he surmised; the girl at the pool was who she was, probably single, and victim to her instincts and wandering eyes. He reached his car, yanked open the door, rolled down his window, and played the rock station KPRI at full blast to drown out the image of the tanned girl.

He sped off back over the bridge to the highway and went east to his apartment, arriving there in a few minutes. He opened the front door and found Ron, as usual, in the kitchen. Since he had been living there, Ron was either barricaded in his room for hours, or cleaning in the kitchen, or eating some type of stock, vegetable soup. He seemed never to enter the living room to watch sports, and John deduced that he did not want to get too close to him for some reason. He assumed it was jealousy that he had a girlfriend and now was getting married which made him uncomfortable.

"Hey, what's happening?" Ron amiably asked, cleaning some dishes.

"Hey, Ron, nothing much. Has anyone called?"

"No, just the ball and chain," he responded with laughter.

"Oh, Ernestine," he gruffly said.

"Yeah, about fifteen minutes ago," he declared as he furiously wiped down the countertop. "So, you two are getting married?"

"Yes," John placidly said. "Soon. Not sure of the date, but I will let you know when I am moving out and give the landlord notice."

"Okay," he responded. "I wish you all the luck. Are you sure you want to go through with it?" he halfheartedly said.

John eyed him, and answered, "Sure I'm sure. It is about time. It has been only three years, and if I don't commit, I will get my ass kicked."

Ron just smiled as he continued wiping the counter. As he leaned over, his hair, parted in the middle, was falling in front of his face. John probed, "So how is the Asian girl?"

"Rose? She is okay. Like I said, she's too much for me. Besides, she is too short." Ron Miller began dancing in the kitchen as his rock music was blaring, with his door open. He started singing, moving, playing an air guitar. John thought he was silly, and could never act like he did: impulsive, pretending to be a star, idle, and lonely. He did not know too much of him in the several months living there, except that he came from Michigan with his parents twenty years ago. He had been working in some mysterious warehouse, forever, maybe ten years in shipping and receiving. He never said his age, but John assumed he was about twenty-eight. He had a dubious face and manner as he talked, showing little emotion, and his voice tended to be nasally. He was a clean freak.

"Rose... that's a funny name for a Vietnamese girl," John commented.

"That's her name," he asserted. "Maybe it was made up. Maybe she is on the run from the law."

"You're kidding," John spat out. "Right?"

"Of course I'm kidding. Can't you take a joke?" He did not add anything, and he did not appear to have any passion for her John wondered if he really went out with her, or was just trying to impress him. John studied him, and tried to decipher what made Miller move, what drove him, what excited him. He decided nothing did but rock music.

"You are home early," Ron added.

"Yes. I decided to call in sick today, tired of shuffling paperwork."

"Just to let you know," he said pragmatically, "someone called a few times and hung up. The last time she gave her name, a Susan something or other."

Aroused, moving to the kitchen, John asked, "Did she say anything or say what she wanted?"

"No," he answered, shaking his head. "No message. Who is she? I thought lover boy was engaged. Playing around on the side, huh," he joked. "You better be careful, dude."

"Oh, I am. It's not that, just someone I knew from college. Maybe it's a reunion." John went back to the living room and calmly sat on the couch in deep thought. "I better call Ernestine. She should be home by now." Ron stood in the kitchen making a sandwich as John dialed the number.

"Hi, honey," she said. "How are you?"

"Great, can't complain."

"You haven't been picking up any girls on the side?" she said jokingly.

"No, of course not," he replied, annoyed.

"Keep your eyes in your head. Remember, we are engaged."

"You always remind me of that. Why?"

Ernestine paused, and added, "A good-looking guy like you... you would be a good catch to some girl."

"Sure. Anyway, I was thinking, this Friday, why don't you come over after work and stay the weekend? We'll have dinner at El Torito."

"Sure! Sounds good!" Ernestine animatedly said. "How was your day?"

Nervous, staring at the roommate in the kitchen, John replied, "Fine, pushing the paperwork. How was yours?"

"Tough. A patient died today of heart failure. A man of only fifty-six; makes you think about life and what is important."

"Yes, I know. I don't take anything for granted. Fifty-six? That is young."

"Yes, but I don't want to talk about that. Let's talk about something positive. Don't forget, we have to pick out a ring this weekend. We can go to J Jessops in the Valley."

Panting, his head up at the ceiling, he said, "Sure, why not."

"Great! You sound a bit down," she prodded. "What's up? Did something happen?"

"No, nothing," he idly said.

"You certainly don't talk much. Did that stupid Susan call again?"

"No, not her. Honey, like I said, I will handle that. Don't worry about her, she's nothing."

Ron continued to listen quietly in the kitchen, as he delved into the fridge for food, and then began furiously wiping the stove top.

"She better be nothing," Ernestine said in a warning tone, "or I will kick your ass... I'm not going to be second fiddle to some dumb white—" She caught herself, and breathed heavily. "Anyway, I am glad it is over; you keep your eyes on me, I told you that before. I am a pretty good catch, even if I say so myself."

"You are, and I love you. Don't forget that," he placidly said.

"Okay, honey, I will let you go. I should be at your place around, let's say, four. I hope your roommate is out so we can have some quiet time. And you may just get some of this chocolate."

John, aroused, replied, "I would like that. Can't wait to slap that behind."

"Bye," she said, and hung up.

John put the receiver down, relieved, and glanced at the kitchen. Ron had moved to his room and shut the door, blaring some intense rock music. John stood in the middle of the living room, planning his weekend and dwelling on the dreaded engagement ring and the cost. He shook his head, said, "What the hell!", and went to his room and shut the door.

# CHAPTER 9

Friday arrived quickly, and Ernestine was excited as she clocked out of the hospital at exactly three fifteen. She sauntered to her car, humming a tune, revved the engine, turned on some disco music by the Bee Gees, donned her fashion sunglasses, and raced home to get her things. In fact, they were already packed by the door, a small suitcase loaded with everything a girl needed: underwear, perfume, two cotton shirts, scarf, black buckle shoes, a white pair of tennis shoes, a sunhat, slacks, jewelry, a small towel, lotion, polish, and the proverbial black clutch purse with a golden chain to round out the attire for the evening.

She arrived home and jumped up the stairs, opened the blinds and windows with the breeze flowing into the apartment, and felt happy and elated. She gathered her things, straightened the apartment, sipped a glass of Chablis, and turned on the music. She sat down carelessly on the couch, fingered her hair using a small mirror, moved her neck, which was tight, crossed her legs and sat in silence. No phone calls, no hospital paging, no monitors, no complaining patients and family members, no death or pain, no nosy doctors, no medication and endless reading of charts and notes, no more oppressive drudgery. She suddenly recalled the last phone call to John, earlier in the week, and his apparent uneasiness. Ernestine Jones stopped drinking the chilled wine, froze, peered out the living room window, and had an uncanny feeling. *What if he is not faithful to me? What if he went out with this Susan girl and had a last fling?* She knew he was faithful, steady, and in the back of her mind she could rely on him; but she could not be sure of some floozy who wanted to recapture past college days' friendships. She knew nothing of this woman and little of John's college experiences, his connections, his thoughts, or any stray phone numbers he kept in his phone book. She wondered what this woman looked like; was she successful, who were her parents? John said little about her, and the prank phone call that day where she hung up sounded suspicious, forced, and maybe he had a subsequent conversation to rekindle old ties. She was not totally sure, convinced, and now that the proposal had been announced, she wanted to sever any or all ties John might have with any woman, or stupid, soppy friends, who may lead him down the wrong path.

She glanced at the clock and called him, saying she was on the way over and could not wait to see him, her voice assured, pleasant, but she was still perturbed about the woman. Her face, after hanging up, was stern, her mood changing to moroseness; she said if she ever saw this woman with him, she would slap her ugly face and knock her down and beat the crap out of her. She was breathing heavily as she thought about this surly woman. *I got too much to lose, have come so far on this journey with this gem of a man, to throw it all away on a woman's instinct, some idiot who doesn't care about anyone or anything. Just have this bitch call the house one more time, and if I am there, I will straighten her little fanny out.*

She grabbed her bag, locked the door and went down to the garage. She decided to switch to happier thoughts of the wedding plans and who to invite. While driving, her estranged father was entrenched in her first thoughts, and he would have to drive out from arid Arizona for the wedding. But did he have to bring that young gold digger with him? Her father had been living with some young, light-skinned woman for years, and she had no career except to look pretty and take his money. Jerry Jones was from the old school, old way of living; now in his sixties, he tended to stay safe along racial lines and attitudes. Although well off, he was still buried in color, in status, in hatred of certain white folks that, he said, "had done him wrong". He commented to her a few years ago, when he found out who she was dating, that if you moved outside of your race, your life would be hard. It was so final, so absolute, and a bit judgmental. Ernestine did not see John as a color, as different, because love had erased all insignificant barriers and labels. Ernestine conjured the idea that you can't predict love, love is where you find it; it's a force stronger than distrust, racial lines, mores, and stilted opinions. They had talked this out many times and were strong in their beliefs, and thought they were indestructible. Her mother would go with the flow of things, she decided. She had been so hurt from Jerry leaving the roost fifteen years ago, with affairs and drinking on the side, she was settled in the thought that any couple could make it; she was open to new ideas, liked everyone who was genuine, and if you didn't try something different, with new struggles and adventures, you would just wind up in the heap of spinsterhood, divorce, and no children to carry on your family name. Many of the people in her street were in this predicament, unmarried, women living at home in their thirties, lost chances, lost loves, divorces, separated with no husband, nothing to kindle that spark which is the essence of life. Many tangibly stopped living, stopped dreaming, stopped reaching out for dates even of their own skin color, lost in space and time, in a limbo of despair, regrets, and settling for less. This was sad to Ernestine as she continued to drive down the highway, the sun directly flashing in her face east, and she surmised that this could have been her, at an early age, and early grave, with the rest of the people on Tanner Street. Each of these houses had a sad story to tell of death, or deception, or drugs tearing apart the fabric of the family, or someone in trouble with the law thrown into prison for years. His mom, she concluded, was another story to be worked upon and pounded into the realization that all people mattered, and that these old notions of roles, your place in life, do not really exist any more for the people in this new generation who were searching for peace.

And that Brenda girl, the sister, rounding out the clan: she is rough around the edges, a little flirty, but she has Ernestine's back; she knew that when she shows up to the wedding, she will be the life of the party, and they will have to carry her out of the reception dead drunk. That is who Brenda is: ebullient, forceful, and adjusts to the situation presented to her. *I may*, Ernestine believed suddenly, *be an example to Brenda to have her take a chance on someone else in her life, someone who has qualities John has, a person who melts in her arms.*

Her eyes began to water in the telling of these reveries, as the Mustang drove over the speed limit to the exit by the apartment complex. "And I need at least a quarter carat ring," she asserted; "something to stare at all the time. I know John will buy me one because he loves me so much."

She arrived at the carport, got her case, and walked up to the apartment door with bright white jeans on, a short-sleeve shirt, shiny black dress shoes, and her purse dangling from her arm. She adjusted her hair, straightened her pants, and rang the bell. He quickly answered the door, so tall, filling the doorway, so serene, with his green eyes glowing, and a smile on his face. "Hello, gorgeous," he said, and they hugged in the doorway and moved to the living room.

"Come on, put your case in the room, honey; we are going to have a good time tonight." He was animated, like a child moving and scurrying around, fixing papers, putting items in the trash. He inhaled her distinct perfume, having a keen sense of smell, and gazed in wonder at his girl, his fiancée, his hands in his pockets, head back, eyes slightly shut, staring at the high heels in the middle of the room, a bracelet hanging loosely from her small wrist, her purse tightly clenched against her body, the sunglasses raised over the top of her head, with a smile on her face that energized the room. "You look amazing, like a movie star, like Diahann Carroll." He added this as she chuckled at the compliment.

He then took the case as she sat down on the couch and fingered a magazine placed on the coffee table: it was one of hers, left from the last visit, an issue of *Vogue*.

The roommate, Ron Miller, was gone, maybe to happy hour, as John craned his head near the room and heard no movement, and the light was off. There was no noise outside, as if everyone had retired for the evening or were out in the streets. John saw this as a sign that he lived in an exclusive complex where manners and high living were enforced.

Putting the case in the room, John came out, and clapped his hands together, announcing, "Well, what do you want to do first?"

She looked up from the magazine, surprised. "First, come over here and kiss me."

He walked over, with one knee bent on the couch, and kissed Ernestine greedily on her soft lips as she grabbed his face. He put his arm around her back, now on top of her. She commented, "Mmm. That is nice. You are a good kisser. I remember when you were bad and shy at it. You sure have changed your ways." Her voice was soft and sexy, and he was entranced listening to the compliment.

"I had a good teacher, and lots of practice." He cupped her neck in his soft hands, searched her body, inhaled the perfume, and kissed her neck.

"Wait, lover boy… we better stop now. We have a dinner date. Where?"

"El Torito, of course. Good Mexican fanfare and the nightclub if you want to stay. That seems to be the happening spot these days. My friends go there a lot."

"And the margaritas?" she added, eyebrows raised.

"Those are pretty good, too. I could use a few."

"Me, too; two drinks max. It has been a long week," she stated.

There was a pause, as Ernestine rose from the couch, her arms folded, a few feet away from him, and queried, "Any updates on anything? Your friends?"

"No," he nervously said, softly. "Nothing, except Brad and I went out to dinner last week."

"What about that woman who called? Is she still bothering you?"

"Nope, that is resolved. I guess…" He said this in a flat monotone voice, and switched. "What time do you want to leave?"

Staring at him, searching his face for reassurance about Susan, she answered, "Any time, in a few minutes. I'm hungry. By the way," she added, pointing to his head, "go shave – your face is a bit rough."

"Always telling me what to do," he said, trailing off into the bathroom. He scanned his face in the mirror, closely, as if he was a surgeon ready to perform a delicate operation. He picked up the electric razor and furiously moved it around his face, head up, then down, in a hurry to trim the stubble. He finished, and Ernestine, with her shoes off, snuck up behind him, put her arms around him like a snake, staring up into his face, and said, "Hey, babe, that's better." She patted his behind a few times and commanded, "Straighten up that curly mess of hair! If I didn't know better, I would think you were half black with that 'fro!"

"I am half black, a white soul brother, smooth, good looking—"

"I know you are now," she interjected, staring at his mop of hair. "I taught you well, cleaned your ass up really good." With emphasis and caring, fixing his collar, pulling his khaki pants up, she complimented him on the nice dress shoes. "Does the belt match the shoes?"

"Yes," he responded, pulling up the shirt and showing the brown belt bought at Macy's. She did recall when they first met, she had to get the country hick, as she called it, out of this student. She took him to a mall in La Jolla, picked out this nice, thin brown belt, a brown turtleneck sweater, and a pair of Stacy Adams shoes; she was his personal designer, his seamstress that day, searching the sale racks, purchasing a small vial of Polo cologne. He was shocked and flattered with it all that someone would care enough to make him look presentable. She trimmed his neck and put some cream on his hair and pronounced he was ready for society: she asserted that one needed to look chic out there in the world where people who are already judging you will be less inclined to do so, and believe you were wealthy celebrities. For Miss Jones, appearance and diction, the choice of words and manners were crucial in presenting an image to the white world that she belonged in that echelon, in the upper-class mentality where cars were waxed, expensive wine was imbibed, good books were read, and soft jazz music was celebrated. It was all about the image. One needed to deceive these crusty white folks to get what you needed and dispel any ideas that you were from the ghetto.

"You smell nice, honey. What is it?" he politely asked.

"Coco Chanel, of course. Only the best."

He nodded his head in assurance and grabbed her in the bathroom and gave her a big hug. His hands traveled down her white jeans and her behind. He patted it lightly.

"Hey, babe, come on. Let go, tiger, control yourself."

"Sure. My car or yours?"

"Let's take mine and go in style." She patted his chest.

They left the apartment, drawing the blinds, and descended the steps to her clean, polished Mustang. "You drive," she directed, flipping the keys to him. "And no rock music, only soul. Okay?" she added.

They climbed into the two-door sports car, rolled down the windows, the air still warm, and started toward the El Torito in the Valley. They talked idly of the work week, of where to get the rings, price ranges, wedding invitations of who to invite in the short list, and those folks to avoid because they wouldn't show up anyway. They described several folks on the list, mentioning faults and attitudes, and those who had good attributes. Now driving, they were dreamers, planners, uncertain of the future, carefree, not really caring if people liked them or not, driving on, telling jokes, poking fun at each other. Ernestine stared at his thin face, the narrow chin, the mustache, the dark brown eyebrows, and his strong hands gripping the steering wheel. The car rumbled in the rush-hour traffic, passing by businesses on the side of the freeway, a mall on the right; they crossed the southside and meandered down a narrow road and came to the restaurant parking lot. This place was nestled behind some commercial buildings and was near the famous, short-lived Playboy Club that lasted only a few years and closed in 1981. John and his best friend Brad, young and vivacious, went there for a drink when it opened, and it was not as exciting and impressive as the image: no Playboy bunnies were scooting around showing off their goods, and they became disappointed. They bought one expensive drink at a small table hugging a wall by some stairs and left deflated.

John carefully parked the car, got out, and opened the passenger door. He helped Ernestine exit the vehicle, grabbing her hand. "Thank you," she said demurely. They were hoping to be noticed by someone in the lot that they had class and elegance. They walked arm in arm the short distance to the wide, pink steps of the restaurant; the buzz, the noise and clatter of plates and glasses could be heard as they entered the lobby.

John said to the receptionist at the booth, head down, soft voice, "Party of two, nonsmoking." He looked around at the rising scene. People were already seated in booths, talking loud, drinks were consumed, and glasses taken away by waitresses; a few patrons were presently inebriated, having arrived earlier in the afternoon. They were seated in a large area of old-fashioned tables and chairs, with red clothes tight around the tabletops, small candles glowing in bowls, and the main bar was just up the concrete steps into the back of the restaurant. This El Torito was frequented by middle-class workers who, after their shift in the Valley, would come here for happy hour, and consume large quantities of chips, salsa, and appetizers. There were some quiet couples and older folks dispersed in the mix of young single people talking idle nonsense about careers, telling inflated stories about boyfriends, sports, their financial assets, and family problems; the stories got better and juicier as the drinks were consumed, heads together, swapping white lies to impress the listeners. The predominantly white crowd was friendly, the bartenders jovial, hoping for large tips, and they were always moving in a frenzy to fill drinks, wash glasses, and hear brief sob stories. The main drinks were large, strawberry margaritas, Mexican beers, scotch, Long Island Iced Tea, rum and Coke, and anything else to make the customers forget their daily troubles.

Once seated, the light dimmed, John and Ernestine immediately ordered two margaritas to celebrate their life and engagement. She was glowing, happy, her clutch bag draped over the chair, leaning forward on the table toward him, hands clasped together, elegant, and in control. He was dressed properly for the occasion, sitting upright, chest out, scanning the crowd, hair combed, and he reached out with his hand to touch and hold her smooth arm. He noticed the red nail polish, no hair was out of place, the clothes clean and pressed; a gold bracelet was on her right arm, and her Cartier watch on the other. He decided she was the best-looking chick in the place.

The drinks arrived shortly, they stared fondly at each other, and John said, "You look great tonight. Thanks for coming here… Well, let's toast to our new life and engagement." He was serious, but struggled with the emotion of his speech and raised his glass. With a pucker on her face,

Ernestine raised her glass toward his, and with a sly smile, said, "Here's to us! May we have a long and happy life filled with children!"

They clinked their glasses, and they could not take their eyes off each other. They were oblivious to any stares of other patrons in that restaurant, believing that there were several admirers in the crowd wishing they were as happy and loving as they were. Their mannerisms and behavior showed it, an example to possibly one person in all the throng that may question the existence of coupling only with someone just like you in skin tone, class, religion, believing that this way of life was safe and the only way to live. After the toast, they ordered two combination plates of Mexican fare, dabbled into the chips, and imbibed the surrounding music.

He was so quiet, suddenly, so she began a conversation. "How was work today?"

"Same as usual. I had to deal with this client who was intoxicated in the office and talking to himself."

"Oh, what did you do?"

"I could not communicate with him, so we got security to escort him out of the building. He was rude and potentially violent."

"Is that a job you want to do? I mean, you could find easier work somewhere else."

"It isn't a problem, and I guess I am used to it. I was destined to work with people. In college, I was fascinated with how people think and behave. I believe that is important."

"You're right, I guess." She fingered her glass, her head down in thought.

"What do you want to do, say, in five years?"

"Not sure, but I think I may pursue fashion or a modeling career. That would be my passion."

"You have the height and features, honey, to do it. You would be perfect; you just need a connection. I bet you could be the next Beverly Johnson."

He was, to her, so cute in the last remark, animated, always supportive, and honest. She sipped her drink, raised her head, flattered, and said, "Thank you. Thank you for everything. I may just do that. Nothing is going to stop me. I have a girlfriend who is in magazine modeling. I may just give her a call. I can't be a nurse forever, too grueling."

John nodded his head, paused, and inquired, "No rush, but you know I am a planner. When should I move out and in with you? I think we should pool our resources and money."

"Immediately; matter of fact, babe, as soon as possible. You don't need to live with that dumb, fat roommate of yours. You are better than that. Live with me; we'll work it out and find the space… but you need to get rid of some of those old, dirty books and clothes. My apartment is too small for all of that; besides, as they say, I need to keep up the standards." She said the last sentence in a cavalier tone, and it reminded John of a recent crime movie where a Black criminal said it to Clint Eastwood that the standards needed to be kept up, as if that really mattered.

He replied, "Of course I plan on cleaning house. But I am a reader, so I am bringing only the hardcover classics with me. I'll leave Ron the old television and whatever else to scrap: that old double bed, the dresser, that yellow recliner."

"What about bank accounts?" she asked with a serious face.

"I don't know, haven't thought about it… I guess to start out it would be a great idea to have two separate accounts to build up savings and one person to pay all the bills. I'm good with finances."

"You are also good at spending money, dear," She replied. "We will figure all of that out later. For now, we need to concentrate on a ring, the reception, the church—"

"The ring," he interjected, grimacing. "How much is that going to cost? I guess we can finance it."

"I could ask my dad for help," she answered carefully.

"If you want, if he would consider it."

"Why not? He could only say no. It's important to a girl to have the best, get what she wants, so I will pick it out at Jessops, and we can make payments on it."

"Great," he answered, as the steaming food plate arrived shortly later, with the Mexican fare; another margarita was ordered for her, and a draft beer for him. John looked at Ernestine and believed she was already tipsy from the last drink, talking loudly, pushing her food around the plate, eating ravenously, winking at him, bossing him around about wedding plans. He tried to tune it out, as he was tired of the planning and the nervousness of the pending event, which was monstrous to him.

They continued to eat quietly at the table, and John saw and heard a group of three youths at a table about five yards away, ogling them, laughing, one pointing a finger, and he believed one of them used the term 'Jungle Bunny' under his inebriated breath. Several empty beer mugs were strewn on the table as they continued to talk; he could not be sure, but the tone of the conversation was derisive. They looked again, and John glowered at them with his mouth full of food. Ernestine continued to chew without even noticing what was happening.

"You see those idiots behind us?" he sardonically stated, pointing his finger.

"Oh, those hicks from Kansas? Yeah, I saw them when we came in. So what?"

"Well, the fat, ugly one I think said 'Jungle Bunny' or something under his breath... I won't stand for that!"

"Wait, John. Keep your seat. They are drunk. Ignore them," Ernestine replied, putting down her fork on the plate.

John, with his arms folded at the table, his back leaning against the chair, gulped his beer as he scowled at the three kids. "I don't like it and their attitude. You can't say crap like that any more. It's not acceptable! If it continues, either I will say something or tell the manager!"

Ernestine picked up her fork, was composed, and replied, "Just eat, sweetheart, and we will move to the bar and forget those jerks. I told you, there are a lot of haters out there."

John Earley, a person hard to rile, thought his beautiful girl did not insult or bother anybody, was friendly, innocent, and now had to endure this crass behavior from guys who couldn't hold their liquor, ugly youths with no girlfriends, school-age punks spewing out hatred and anything that came into their warped minds to get their jollies. John shook his head in disgust and said to himself, *What asses; how embarrassing it is to have, now in 1982, numskulls like these three in the world trying to create havoc when their silly lives are not complete: probably they are some pampered rich kids, their attire shows it, trying to be preppy, who never have to worry or struggle just to make a living; mama's boys, yes, who are probably living in fancy homes getting an allowance from daddy each week.*

For men like John, now, this day, after three years of dating Ernestine, he realized where his bread was buttered, thinking of this phrase often as she reminded him of it. For loyal white men that dated or married Black women, they were enraptured with chocolate girls, in all shapes and sizes; to some it was an obsession hard to explain, a worshipping of the regal, dark sirens that kept calling them back; their world had changed forever, they would not go back to white women, they loved every inch of their dark shapes, the shiny, clean, maintained skin, the fancy hairstyles, curls and braids, and the jewelry to accent the skin tone, the sensuous lips to kiss, their shapely legs, firm posteriors, the way these Black girls carried themselves, the smooth talk, coy looks, their forcefulness in a pinch, these women unrealized and misunderstood. John dwelled on this in the few seconds staring at the stupid boys.

They finished the delightful, heavy meal, paid the bill, and John suggested they get one drink for the road at the bar. "Okay, but just one," Ernestine answered uneasily, a little drowsy.

They left the table, and John, passing the three young men with their heads down, gave them a glare and said, "Jerks!' and moved on.

She grabbed his right arm, a little unstable, her high heels clicking on the concrete surface, and they walked up the steps to the inner bar area, now crowded, noisy, with its small, circular dance floor. They plopped down on two red bar stools and ordered two Coors Lite beers. The music was blasting some tune from the Gap Band, and Ernestine's head swayed to it, her arm in his, her other hand playing with her hair.

"Got to go to the restroom," she asserted. "Back in a second." She got up and walked sexily down the steps to the bathroom around the corner of the bar and disappeared. John followed her, making sure she did not slip on the smooth surface of the floor, and he peered around the entrance to make sure the three surly youths were not there. They had left their table with mugs and food strewn everywhere, with one napkin on the floor. He went back to his seat, drank his beer, and stared ahead at the bar with all its lights, glasses, and bottles. Two young women presently came in and sat down on two stools around the edge of the bar, attractive, alive, one white woman with sandy blonde hair and the other a thin girl of Persian descent with long, straight hair down her back. They were in casual attire and were laughing close together, and the Persian girl glanced across to him, eyes that were dark and beautiful and seemed to admire him. She smiled, and then looked away and continued talking to the blonde woman, who just spurted out words, her mouth visibly open, her face slightly red, with a scarf around her neck. She reminded him of Heather Locklear or Donna Mills. The Persian girl, with a long, aquiline nose, mid-twenties, was interesting, he surmised, and he drank with his head down, and glanced at her with his eyes up. He asked himself, *What is she like? Does she date outside of her culture? Is she progressive?*

Ernestine came back to the bar, freshened, with more lipstick on, and sat down next to him. She patted his arm, noticed the two women, and remarked, "Those are two attractive women over there."

He replied, unaffectedly, "Yeah, sure."

She snickered. "You are supposed to say no, stupid." Hitting his arm, she added, "I keep telling you to just stare at me."

"You know you are the coolest girl on the planet. I don't need to keep reminding you, do I?"

Tartly, she responded, "Yes you do, and don't forget it."

They sipped their drinks as Ernestine studied the two girls still sizing them up. "Do you want to head out?" he cautiously asked.

"Yes, let's finish the beers. I would like to go back to your pad and you never know, you might get lucky," she hinted, drooling over him, rubbing his arm.

John, excited, gulped the last of the suds, staring at her, noticing still the perfect attire, the composure, the subtle, smooth movements of her hands and body towards him, closer and closer. "Let's go, babe," she asserted.

They left the crowded, smoky restaurant, people scampering in, the noise elevated, and got to the car in the fading twilight and drove carefully home to avoid the police. A Donna Summer song was playing on the radio, and Ernestine was mumbling words to it. She continued to hum and softly sing most of the way home. They arrived at the complex, parked in a space, and slowly walked up the steps, embracing, holding, laughing, joking, poking each other, talking about the evening's festivities. They had quickly forgotten the surly youths at the restaurant, their minds were on other, more personal adventures. John opened the front door, trying to listen to any noise in the unit: the roommate's door was closed, and no sound was heard.

"Come on, honey," he said quietly, patting her back. They locked the front door, entered the large living room, and drew the blinds. She took off her hoop earrings, saying, "Go get undressed and lay on the bed. You know how you like it."

He liked her directness, her assertiveness, and without a word, removed his clothes and lay on his back, staring at her. Shoes off, she haphazardly removed her pants, wiggling them off, her shirt next, and then her underwear, and it was thrown everywhere in his room. Her face was determined. He could scarcely breathe, and he relished her shapely silhouette in the rising dark. She smiled and scooted to the bed, sitting on the edge, and softly whispered, "Now for your little treat."

John was nearly shocked by all of this as he continued to lay comfortably on the mattress. She began fondling his extension, her eyes down, her eyelashes noticeable, eager, for a few moments. Without a further word, she climbed on top of him, positioning herself. John hurriedly grabbed the side of her legs as Ernestine pressed her hands on his hairy chest. Their eyes were half closed, breathing became short, as they were in unison, in rhythm, moving, feeling. John put his hands on her rising breasts; they were slow, patient, knowing that this was a perfect day of their marriage proposal. She bent down and kissed his lips and nuzzled his neck, and he, in rising passion, grabbed her behind to pull her towards him. In their ecstasy, they couldn't fully believe this impulsive romp was happening and, at any moment, the roommate could barge into the house to disturb them.

When it was over, they lay side by side on the bed, with a sheet over them. Her hand was on his neck, and he put his arm around her. She finally said, after a moment, peacefully, "Gosh, that was great."

"Yes," he idly answered, breathing out, kissing the top of her head. "I am glad you came over."

"Me, too," she calmly added. "I like what you did in the restaurant, standing up to those fools who insulted me. I appreciate that."

"I would do it again in a minute. I hate those type of guys who think they are superior to everyone else. Those types of idiots get into trouble and lead stupid, shallow lives."

They thought about the event for a few seconds, and she added, "We can have bacon and eggs in the morning."

"Why not? I have them. I'll cook up a special breakfast for you."

They lay in the bed for a while, watching John's small television on the dresser, and drifted off to sleep around eleven o'clock. They were spooned together.

# CHAPTER 10

John woke early, around six, shivering on this cool June morning, and went to the kitchen to make some coffee. He dwelled on last night's dinner and rendezvous at his apartment, shaking his head. Ernestine was still asleep in the bed, in the process of waking up. He put on some strong coffee, snatched two frying pans for breakfast and began to whistle. He opened the kitchen blinds to the rising gray morning, shook his head again, downed two aspirins, and got the food from the refrigerator.

At this moment, the phone rang, and he jumped. He let it ring one more time, cursing under his breath, and ran to the phone. He said, disturbed, "Hello."

"Is this John?"

"Yes, who is this?" he asked, miffed, eyes furrowed.

"Anna, Anna Cohen. Sorry to call you so early this morning."

"Oh, Anna! How the heck are you?"

"Great… I have some bad news." She trembled, her voice quivering. "Susan has passed away."

John paused in trepidation, taking a step backwards, his mouth open, and finally spoke. "She passed away. What are you talking about?"

"Two days ago, I went to check on her. I was concerned the last time I saw her, that she may have had a breakdown. I had this premonition that something tragic was going to happen and I wanted to stop it. I went to the house and the owner answered the door. She was all shaken up and stated that the police were there, and they think it was a suicide."

"Suicide! I can't believe this!" He was in a fog, his hand rubbing his temple. "That is not like her; she was so young and had her whole life in front of her."

"Listen, the owner told me that they found her dead on the floor, by her bed, and all these pills were strewn about the room, and a bottle of vodka half empty on the dresser. I told you she was using drugs, and that explains her behavior. John, the room was taped off when I was there. It is all so scary to me."

"Anna, I don't know what to say. But I guess that explains a lot of things."

"What do you mean?" she pleaded. "You knew, too?"

"Yes, Anna. About a week ago, Susan called me for some reason, and hung up the phone, no explanation, no message. She had been calling my house several times and even drove out to my parking lot like she was casing the place. Is that not strange behavior?"

"Creepy, if you ask me… It must have been drugs or some illness," Anna concluded. "She was wired the last time I saw her."

"That is not all," he replied, bellowing. "She called me to meet her at the Revelle Library under the tree, the same one we used to hang out. When I got there, she looked demented, didn't make sense, said she loved me… I just left her there. I couldn't afford to handle that crap."

"I know, I know, John. I am sorry you had to go through all that odd behavior. Thank God she didn't hurt anyone. It is so sad."

"I am glad you called. We can only move on and forgive her… What's new in your world?"

Anna answered, tentative, "Well, I began my student teaching on campus and love it. The books, the research, the students, it brings back memories of those college days. You know, you should pursue a teaching career or research."

"No," he replied, flatly. "I am just going to stick with my treasured books, and the classics in my spare time. That is enough for me. I don't have the energy and fortitude to teach a bunch of students."

"On a brighter note, the big question… when is the wedding date and how is Ernestine?"

"Great. We haven't set a date yet. When we do," he said nervously, "I'll send you an invitation. Would you like to come?"

"Sure. If I am in town, I'd love to."

"Then it's settled." There was an awkward hiatus. "Well, thanks for calling me." He added, "Man, that was bad news about Susan. I wish it never happened. I hope you are handling it okay."

"Yes, it is a shock. The best thing to do is to keep busy and focus on good thoughts. John, take care, and God bless."

He said goodbye and hung up the phone, in deep thought, drank some coffee and went back to the bedroom.

Ernestine was at the edge of the bed, getting dressed. She looked up and inquired with fear in her voice, "Who was that? You look like you saw a ghost."

John's face was pale, depleted, his hands were out. "Susan," he stammered, "that girl Susan… they found her dead in her room. A suicide, they think."

"That's terrible," she replied. "You never want to hear about that. Dead." She was shaking her head, hands by her mouth.

John went to the edge of the bedroom doorway, one hand on top of the frame. "I have never been exposed to death, someone dying. It doesn't seem real to me. It's over, anyway." He went to the living room, head down, as she followed him out, her arms folded.

She caught up to him and put an arm around him. "Are you sure you are okay?"

"Yes, I will be fine. For her to do that, she must have been sick and desperate. How do you kill yourself? A college graduate, good family background, only twenty-four or so; how do you make sense of it? I guess you can't."

"You can't, darling. Where I come from, the community I lived in, people were dying all the time: drugs, shootings, stabbings, heart attacks. You become used to it after a while."

"I guess you do." He paused, looked at her, breathed deeply, and continued, "Let's forget all this. I have an idea. Why don't we forget all of this bullcrap and go up the coast? How about LA and the Garment District?"

"Sure," she demurely answered. "I am off work today, let's do it."

"First thing, I will make a quick breakfast, put some drinks in the ice chest, and then we are out of here!"

John moved quickly like a cheetah all over the apartment, with a serious demeanor, driven to dispel Susan from his mind. They ravenously ate the bacon and sunny-side eggs with the rest of the coffee, while Ernestine looked fondly at John to decipher his mood and feelings. She patted his back on the bar stool chair as she continued to eat. The roommate never came out of his room. Gosh, maybe he is staying with Rose, the Vietnamese, girl, John surmised. They put their clothes together and she asked, "You are sure you are going to be all right, babe?"

"Never better," he tersely answered, then switched. "I am sorry I got you involved with all of this. It was nothing, really nothing, like I told you." He peered off into the lighted kitchen window, and continued, "Sad, real sad. Anyway, as they say, life is for the living. Let's go."

He moved her away from the kitchen, carrying a duffel bag, the ice chest, two sweaters, cash and credit cards, donned his sunglasses, and closed the windows and drapes in the apartment.

They got into the blue Pontiac hatchback, first checking oil, tires, and cleaning the windows; the car had a full tank of gas. He drove to the highway to head up north on the 5 freeway. Despite John's disposition and mood, Ernestine looked at him with fondness. She decided to be impeccable today for him, to raise his spirits; she had her signature black hair, parted on the side, flowing in the wind, with dark brown eyelashes, red rouge on her prominent cheeks, red/orange lipstick, and gold earrings. Her outfit was smart: a purple short-sleeved shirt with the collar turned up, the sweater dangling from her thin neck, white short pants, and new white Puma tennis shoes. Her voice as she talked to him was even, smooth, assured, her brown eyes were alive and caring. They did not mentioned Susan at all. They were through with it, the ugliness, the madness, the absurdity of it all. She thought of him, last night's romantic encounter vivid in her mind, his strong, lean body and hands caressing her shoulders and posterior, his tongue, skillful, and touching all the right places, the embrace, the clenching, the total passion that was theirs, their secret, their moment. She asserted, she knew she had a good one here, a soulmate, intelligent, soft-spoken man with the noticeable Roman nose, pointed chin, and tense muscular arms. He would be twenty-four tomorrow.

While driving on the freeway, she asked, "I assume you told your dad the good news?"

"No, not yet. I hinted at it the last time I saw him a month ago. He was happy about it."

"Good. I like him despite his faults. He is so stuck up sometimes… rigid. He has not said one bad thing about me or us. I like that."

"I wish more people we know felt the same way. It's like a great mystery to them, like we are some side show, a spectacle, an anomaly they are trying to figure out."

"I like being a mystery," she confidently replied. "Gives them something to think about. No matter what, we stay strong." Her body was leaning towards him as he endlessly drove the small car north to Los Angeles. She continued, "I like your black shirt and white shorts. You're hip."

"Thanks," he said, shaking his head, fixated on this slang word 'hip', and realizing it was a compliment to be so cool. He finally rejoined, "You are not so bad yourself," driving with one arm on the wheel, glancing at her, gliding in between cars. He added solemnly, "Thanks for going with me. I needed to clear my head from the news."

"Sure," she pleasantly said, scanning his body. "By the way, did you like last night?"

Surprised, he said, "Yes, always, of course." With an affected stare, he added, "You are my queen, you know that."

She smiled at him, her head leaning to one side, her arm out touching him, patting his right arm. They drove past exit after endless exit, passing Carlsbad, Oceanside, with endless hills and trees with a vast stretch of no houses, the state beach at San Onofre, the dome towers like spaceships, then past the migrant checkpoint, veering north along winding roads, fast, picking up speed, the midmorning, now sunny, the ocean not far away, majestic, blue, still. A few boats could be seen, and all around, tinged, green and brown hills, passing a few restaurants like Jimmy's and Denny's, then small outlets just off the exits. Ernestine kept pointing out to John various sites, landmarks, questioning what they were, commenting on them, excited, happy to be out of town. They were indeed safe, grateful to forget all the madness of their lives, to forget stupid, ignorant people they had recently met, in the bar, on their jaunts, snide remarks so searing from family members and strangers, or the silence of passing strangers, all these things, in this San Diego world, seemingly trying to judge, to hold them back from their destiny and enchanted love. It was all so silly and pointless, as these youths had the verve, the energy to believe that they were indestructible.

"Where to first?" he asked near San Juan Capistrano.

"We said the Garment District, right? We can get some good deals on some clothes there. We may even find a wedding dress."

This fashion district in Downtown LA, was opened in 1972, and by 1982 comprised over five hundred retail outlets from Seventh to Twelfth Street, and was an area known for great bargains on wholesale items such as purses, clothing, luggage, electronics, jewelry; anything you could fit in a house was there for the asking, and bargaining. Some of these items were 'knock-offs', not being original but much less expensive. It was an area of energy, of movement, of mass crowds on the weekend, catering to the Spanish population in tow with children searching the toy tables, the famous Santee Alley down this long, narrow strip where higher-end items were waiting for eager purchasers.

"You said you wanted a wedding dress there? So soon?" John queried.

"Maybe; if not, let's just splurge on a nice Louis Vuitton purse or a pair of leather sandals for the summer."

"That sounds better than a wedding dress, so early, makes me a bit nervous. Do you want to take a trip this summer?"

"No, not in the mood for one. I think we should concentrate on the wedding plan; there is so much to do. And the expenses, what do you think?"

"It's your call, honey. I tend to agree with you. There are a lot of details to work out... it seems so overwhelming if you think about it."

"Not really. If you are in love, it doesn't really matter. We will make it perfect, and people will be talking about it for years." She shook her head with the dark sunglasses on and she stared at the crushing traffic. John mused about her last statement that it would be remembered for years, and was uncertain of certain people's reaction to the ceremony, and assumed it was just jitters.

They were now, after a period of silence, past the city of Irvine, just entering the last stretch to the Downtown District, the lanes narrowing, cars halting and then accelerating, rude people passing each other, cutting drivers off, in this big city; it was fast-paced, different, stressful, and you could feel people's energy and mannerisms in the way they recklessly drove past cars. John, presently, took his time, concentrated, pressed the small car on as Ernestine sipped a Coke from the cooler. She then opened and thumbed a copy of *Glamour*, with a Black woman on the cover. The jazz music was softly playing, the windows rolled down, and the rumble noise was heard from trucks and sports cars enveloping the space.

Oddly, breaking the silence, he asked with a smile, "Have you read any good books lately?"

"Books?" she responded, frowning at him. "Books. Let's see... I did pick up a copy of *Giovanni's Room* by Baldwin, read that, but it was depressing. I don't read much any more since college. I should. I did start a book by Jane Austen, *Emma*, but found it a bit dry."

"Oh, Austen, good writer," he affirmed. "I recently got a copy of *Lord Jim* by Conrad, and it's fascinating. It has a sad ending where he dies."

She did not seem to listen or care, and just nodded and hummed while still scanning the magazine.

"You are so intellectual," she said with quiet emphasis. "You should have been a writer or something."

"Maybe some day. I did think about it in college, but life caught up with me. I was driven to make money and start a career and get out of my mom's house that was so stifling. It is sad you can't develop your creative side and pursue your passion, and you must answer to some stupid boss and push papers all day." He shook his head in disgust as he asserted this. He was torn between his dream world and reality, and what he wanted to do, and instead had to do, the obligations, the regrets of not pursuing a Master's degree, teach, and write books; he saw this world as vital, exciting, and now, forgotten. The only way to appease and bring it back was, for him, to read his treasured classics, history and biographies of great men and women.

"You should have my job, babe. Nursing is no joke. You put up with rude patients, rude doctors, people sick all around, coughing and excreting fluids, and when a patient dies, you wonder what is the purpose? Are you really helping people or prolonging their agony with all these drugs to keep them going. Sounds silly and trite, doesn't it? Shit, the administration wants to push sick people out of bed spaces as quickly as they can for insurance reasons, or they have no money, and some more serious case is waiting for the room. It is like a hotel centered around money, and I think it is insane."

John Earley understood this; he was in the helping profession, too, where it appeared that paperwork was more important than clients' lives and the issue of poverty and despair seemed to dominate his office, and he had few solutions to give. The solutions were based around funding and criteria that people had to meet, and many were turned away at the door due to lack of space or services. "Progress, what's that?" he barked. "The system is set up to keep people down, keep minorities in their place. I know what you are feeling."

"We are talking the same language," she answered. "We are, as they say, cut from the same cloth. If these helpless people did not have us, where would they be? In the streets? No one cares for anyone any more; individuals, today, are so selfish at times, so self-centered, chasing money as their god, stepping over folks along the way. I used to be enthusiastic about my job, once. Black people, especially, have it rough, passed up for promotions, ignored, told to stay in their place; you would think things would change in the last thirty years or so, but it continues, the struggle they call it… Here we are, giving lectures on society and the social condition. It all doesn't matter, anyway." She stopped here, before getting upset, rapidly turning the magazine pages, and staring out the passenger window, her elbow on the door.

"You have a good point," John said, energized by the debate, pointing his finger ahead of him. "Even though we are so different, we are the same. I remember my first day at college, lost on campus and running to my first lecture. I got there and it was a class on Anthropology taught by this Indian professor in this large auditorium, and what he said was so valid. He talked about this theory of the psychic unity of mankind, which basically means all people of all cultures have the same mental makeup... I found that fascinating and always remember it."

"You see," she emphasized, "you should have been a writer, a scholar."

"Maybe. The point I'm making is, like us, we came together at a time where we needed a connection, despite our differences, despite what people and the world said. It is sort of eerie."

"Yes, I said this before. We found each other in the chaos of our lives and stupid, dysfunctional families; we were just trying to break away, be free, free from prejudice, rules, parents telling us what to do... I am so glad I found you." She started to tear up, her face shaking as she stared out the windshield into the glare and smog, cars continuing to push onwards, watching the exits carefully for their destination. The shopping tour, now, did not mean as much as the connection and sharing of ideas that transpired on the trip, a freeing of feelings and emotions of things suppressed forever. Their bond was so intense, a saw could not cut through it.

"You know, Ernestine, it was all ordained from the beginning of time."

She stared at him in his uncanny assertion. "What do you mean?"

"Ordained, by God. I believe this in my soul. He brought us together. In our lives, everything, every event has a purpose, right? I recall when I was young, in New York, my grandfather took me fishing with my brother on this long pier. I must have been around ten, carrying this thick, black pole, and I was right next to this young Black kid about my age. We smiled at each other, began talking about the fish, when my angry grandfather, who was married to an Italian woman, came up to me, pushed me away from the kid, and said, 'Get away from that N-!' I was startled, and after that I began to question things, my world, ideas about race and prejudice. I saw my grandfather after that day as a hypocrite; before he was my idol, after that he was a flawed man."

"That is some story. I got mine also," she added with agitation. "Look at my dad: a sinner, with a loose woman, leaving the kids behind now fifteen years, fifteen long years of suffering, especially for mom. And when he found out I was dating a white man, he flew off the handle, over the phone, annoyed, telling me to get rid of you and go back to Spencer, my old boyfriend. He basically said it was not going to work out, and these so-called interracial relationships would end up in failure. My own father, you would think he would want his children to be happy... Yes, he was a hypocrite, too, as mom caught him shacking up with white women in the neighborhood. I know it is the past, but it is hard to forgive and forget."

"It is crazy if you think about it," John pursued. "Destiny is real, strong, people sense if someone is caring and right for them. I wish the rest of the world believed the same way. But they don't. They go on leading shallow, unexciting lives."

The diatribe ended for a minute. The car neared the exit for the Garment District and veered off on San Pedro Street and a slight decline towards Maple Street to locate parking. He found a small, run-down lot for a five-dollar fee.

"Well, honey, we made it in one piece," he said, exhaling and stretching. "Let's go and have some fun."

They stared at the tall brick buildings around them, their necks craning up, and wondered what type of businesses were conducted in them, or were they abandoned? They walked hand in hand to the main street, where a faint noise was heard from the vendors and cars traveling down the streets. They passed by some homeless camped out on the sidewalks with portable tents and tarps to cover them, as if they were hiding or ashamed of their circumstance. Ernestine cringed as she went by them, and grappled John's arm for protection. There was a faint smell of urine and mustiness in the stale air on this main street, and they quickly walked to the booths and shops to forget the misery they had seen, people talking to themselves, a few begging for money, some in idleness, flat stares at them, one Mexican woman with no legs, moving on a low, flat cart, trying to sell cheap jewelry. One skinny Black girl, about twenty, passed them with dolphin shorts on and a tube top, swaggering her posterior and with a surly smile. The vendors had tables out on the sidewalks, plying their trade of coats, shoes, purses, watches, belts, trinkets, toys, clothing racks, and some of the vendors were aggressive, almost touching them as they passed, desperate for a sale. Some were polite, silent, as if they had been doing this line of work for years and were apathetic about their business. Stares and more stares, then words in Spanish were yelled out in desperation, and street vendors cooking food would say the price to attract hungry shoppers to indulge.

Ernestine stopped at a small table, pulling on John's arm, where a Mexican man, wearing cheap gold chains and jewelry, was selling purses strewn all about. John eyed him and thought he was a circus worker with all the fake jewelry, slick-back hair, and phony smile and mannerisms. She saw a brown Gucci purse on the table, examined it, and said, "Señor, how much?"

"One hundred dollars," he politely replied "Good quality, miss." The seller quickly scanned John to determine if he was rich and could increase his prices.

"How about eighty dollars, cash?" she insisted. She had the money out in one hand; the vendor thought for a few seconds and, shaking his head, said, "Okay. Do you want a bag cover?"

"Yes, please... Hey, honey, what do you think of the purse?"

"Great, just your style," he animatedly answered. "Just add it to the collection," he commented, and got a mean stare from her.

They left the table as the vendor tried to push another purse on Ernestine, who waved him off, and they continued north on Maple Street a few blocks and entered a crushing zone of people moving in all directions, blocking the sidewalks to finger items, cars on the street attempting to find parking in structures with men out in the middle of the street, with flags waving them in for a sale, five or ten dollars for the day, yelling, barking, smiling, directing with fervor. The scene was lively, people passing money to vendors, receiving change, the crowd with a collective murmuring sound, a buzz, cars screeching and honking their horns, individuals racing everywhere, children running down the street, trying to catch up to parents, couples linked arm in arm as if this was the big date, the outing of a lifetime, excited, anticipating finding that special item among the racks for a few dollars so they can gloat, later, to their friends and say they paid full price at Nordstroms. It was all a silly game of cat and mouse, talking the desperate sellers down in price to get what they wanted. Some of the conversations were direct, surly, tense, and it went on all day until late afternoon.

John espied a nice brown wallet at one stand and paid forty dollars for it. "Man, that was a good deal," he said, examining and smelling it to make sure it was leather. "In the store," he commented, "that wallet would have been two hundred dollars for a Louis Vuitton."

"Come on, handsome, let's check out the Santee Alley," Ernestine added.

While at the corner, waiting for the light to change, a woman tapped her shoulder. She turned around and with a big smile, exclaimed, "Barbara Gillam. Is that you? Hey, girl!"

"Yes, it's me! How are you doing?" This Barbara Gillam was about thirty-five, a Black woman with Indian heritage who had a wide face; she was divorced, about five feet five, had plain features with dark brown plastered hair like in the style of the sixties; she had on a red, plaid dress, a cheap watch, and Doctor Scholl-style shoes.

"What are you doing here?" Ernestine inquired, hugging her.

"I live here, silly. After leaving that nursing job two years ago, I moved in with my parents in Encino. That was a change, and it was hard to pull up stakes. But, as you know, I hated that job with all the stress… it wasn't for me." She said all this quietly as if nothing really mattered, with no emotion.

"What do you do now?" Ernestine asked.

"I work in retail at Nordstroms in a fancy mall catering to the wealthy. I want the good life. I'm sorry, this is my husband, Chen."

From behind her, a young Chinese man, small, with glasses, came up tentatively and introduced himself. "Hello, I'm Chen, pleased to meet you." He extended his small hand in a weak handshake.

"I'm Ernestine. Oh, guys, this is my fiancé, John," she said, pushing him up in front of her. John said hello, bowing his head, extending a firm handshake to Chen, and forcing a smile.

"My, he is handsome, Ernestine. You got a good one there," Barbara added, looking him up and down, her lips puckered, a frown on her face in admiration. He felt presently nervous and like an animal on display at the zoo. He grimaced and had his hands in his pockets.

"You know, honey," Barbara insisted, "you need to quit that dumbass job and relocate. There is too much to do here in the city. It has everything. And the pay is good."

"I have been talking about it with my fiancé recently, and I may pursue a fashion or modeling career. Nursing is okay, but you are right, it is full of stress and heartache. I don't want to wind up a fat, ugly, broken-down woman at forty-five with sore feet. Besides, I could make a fortune in modeling with the right connection."

"You certainly have the looks for it. Just do it, and don't look back. Just leave."

Ernestine studied what Barbara Gillam said. She concluded that Barbara was always a rebel, never satisfied, always changing friends, and since her divorce, a bit of a troublemaker on the job, and she had this notion that the hospital fired her for being late or too chummy with personnel or patients. She fed her a story of quitting and did not believe a word of it. She was that type of woman, in the new age, liberated, aggressive, no scruples, and was a gypsy moving from career to career, one idea after another, one friend dumped to find another, and she had no remorse.

"I might just do that," Ernestine said in appeasement. "I may just move to LA after the wedding and start over. It is a big step, and I must really think about it. My roots and family are in San Diego, and the move would hurt them."

Chen, meanwhile, chimed in, asking John, "Well, John, how do you like the city?"

"Good. I have been here before, but first time down here. Got some good deals already."

"Good, good," Chen said in a monotone voice. He had a baby face, was clean shaven, with short black hair and small brown eyes. He probed, "What do you do in San Diego?"

"Social work," he asserted confidently. "I work with the homeless and poor."

"Interesting; sounds rewarding. You must have past several homeless on your way down here. We have got quite a problem with them."

"Yes, I know. I have read several studies on the population here. But to answer your question, the job is good. Some days are tougher than others… How about yourself?"

"I work in electronics and computer repair. To most people it sounds boring, but to me it is challenging."

"Nice, that's a good skill to have." He did not want to continue talking to him, because he seemed to be so different, strange, and unnerving. Ernestine and Barbara were animatedly talking about the old days at the hospital, laughing, reminiscing on special patients or staff members.

With a surly face, Barbara delved, "Is that Rico Lombardi still working at Sharps? He is some hunk, if you know what I mean. He tried to get me out on a date with him… too pushy. I turned him down."

Listlessly playing it off, Ernestine replied, "Rico is still there, a lost puppy. He's got so much talent and looks, he should be settled and married by now. I believe he has an inferiority complex."

"Good label. You know what?" Barbara said under her breath, hand cupped to her mouth, "I think he is gay, and all of this bravado and talking about women is a front. There is something about him, too quiet about his personal life, don't you think?"

"I could give a shit. I have my man," Ernestine defiantly said. "And no one is going to take him away from me." She said this for effect to let Barbara know her place and to quit staring at him.

"Ain't that the truth," Barbara placidly uttered. "But keep an eye on him, he's real good looking, like, you know, a Robert Redford type. You know how men are; you been through it with that Spencer character... Does he cheat, you think?"

"Are you stupid? Of course he's faithful; he's a good, steady guy that loves me. You may have been out with some cheating homeboys, but not me. I gave up that lifestyle long ago." Ernestine became perturbed about the insinuation of cheating, as if the friend expected or wanted it to be, so she could feel her pain. She found Barbara a little crass and forward.

"Just checking. You know what happened to me with Craig – he dumped me after finding some white chick to screw behind my back for six months, and I never suspected him. That was five years ago, and I never got over that one."

"How did you find out?"

"It is funny you ask that," Barbara said in a seething tone, her face serious as if she could kill someone. "On a Saturday, he said he was going to watch the game at the sports bar down the street. Well, he had been ignoring me in the bedroom, so do you know what I did? I followed his black ass in my car down a few streets, trailing far behind, to this duplex where he got out and waltzed up to this door and entered. I parked about thirty yards away, shocked, wondering what he was doing, lying about the sports bar. I got out of my car with the spare crowbar from the trunk, went to the door and knocked. Some ugly, fat white chick, strung out on drugs, answered the door and I saw Craig in the background, his shirt off, drinking a beer. I yelled at his ass to get the hell out of there and told Miss Susie if I ever see her again with him, I will wrap that crowbar around her skull. That is the truth. After that, I was through with him and got a divorce. Good riddance!"

"What a story," Ernestine said in shock. "I know that is tough… but you got a good man now, married and all. Just hold on to him. By the way, where did you meet your husband?"

"At a strip club," Barbara responded with no affectation or guilt. "It is a great place to pick up single men, of course."

"A strip club, are you kidding me?" Ernestine replied, squinting, mouth open in disgust, arms folded.

"Yes, there are a million clubs up here. After work one day, late, I decided to go and checkout the scene. Hey, I said, what have you got to lose? I went in and there was this

Chinese guy, Chen, by himself, sitting on a bar stool with all these cute girls shaking their fannies, eating finger food, and sipping a beer. The seat next to him was empty, so I waltzed right up to him, straightened my hair, and sat down pretty as you please. He was not even watching the nude girls; boy, his eyes were on me. We talked awhile, he liked what he saw, and we exchanged numbers."

"Barbara, you are some wild chick. A strip club?"

"Sure, why not? He was professional, made good money in computers. We dated for six months, and the rest is history. I am not the one to live alone. He treats me right."

"Whatever," Ernestine said, distracted. She immediately flashed back in time to her rendezvous with John in a rundown hotel and the affair. She saw this as impulsive and a bit dirty. She would not judge the former nurse because she said to herself that strange things happen to people; John was right, there is a destiny, a plan for people's lives that defies logic.

"Ready, honey," Barbara said to Chen, who continued to jabber with John on the proverbial sports scene. "Time to go," she demanded with force. Everyone said their goodbyes, and Barbara quietly added, "If you want, I will give you my number. Next time you are in LA, give me a call. We'll see the sights."

"Sure, okay," Ernestine dubiously said, and was handed a small piece of paper with the number. "Bye, you all," Barbara said as she tugged Chen with her, crossing the street on Pico Boulevard.

"Chen seems like a nice guy," John surmised. "Smart, real smart. But a bit of a nerd, though."

Ernestine did not hear what he said. She stared at Barbara Gillam as she moved across the street, shuffling slightly, a little too old before her time. Time, what is that? Is it so important? People are more important in what they stand for than aging. She assumed this Barbara Gillam had drastically changed in the two years she had left the hospital. She was not sure if it was better, though; she seemed to be in pain as she walked, separated from her husband, no hand holding, and she yelled at him as they crossed the street. She thought Chen was a silent prude, and he stared at her like she was an exhibit while she conversed with Barbara; he would glance at John and quickly stare back at her, studying her. He was standing behind his wife the whole time and had these incisive blank eyes, with no emotion and no life in them. She really did not care about him or Barbara, and concluded it was just a chance incident to relive old glory days. But would Ernestine Jones become like them in a few years after marriage? Would their love become stale and apathetic? It was only a moment's thought and she dismissed it. She forced a smile at her beau and said, "Let's shop and then grab some lunch. I'm starving!"

She guided him on through the rising crowd, crossing dirty, cracked streets filled with puddles against the curbs, pawing items stack on tables. She impulsively bought a pair of leather sandals made in Mexico. She was now loose, ebullient, forgetting Barbara, and she kissed John on his cheek. John guarded her and they moved and received dirty stares from some of the Spanish men, hardened, wrinkled, beaten down by laborious work and trauma. Their faces told a story of past hurts, passed troubles, past problems with the law, and endless discrimination by the dominant culture. John held her hand tight in the crushing crowd, as if they were a prison gang chained together, inseparable. He did not trust anyone in this new environment.

"Where do you want to eat?" he asked.

"Over there," she replied, pointing to a Mexican restaurant, the building made of a pinkish stone, battered and dirty over time.

"We could go to a nice restaurant somewhere else," he suggested.

"No, why travel? Let's taste some of the local food and have a few brews, okay?"

They picked out a few more shirts for her, a scarf, and several cheap t-shirts. The couple crossed at the corner, and entered an eatery called Panchos, ordered two plates of tacos with beans and Tecate beer. They pawed their bags of treasures, commented on the trip and sights, and some of the odd people in the environment. They sat in a booth, side by side, John rubbing Ernestine's leg, and she was playing with his curly hair. The food was good, and they ate ravenously; she winked at him, studying his face, hoping he did not dwell on the tragic Susan Swanson, gone, lost to oblivion. He kissed her on the neck, and she was receptive.

"Must be the food. Calm down, lover boy," she said close to his face. After a few minutes, her arm enwrapped in his, and, pushing his chin up with her hand, in a sultry voice, she added, "Finish up and we will head back to the ranch."

They guzzled two more beers in this hole-in-the-wall place inhabited by the Mexican folk and a few white tourists with children who blared and ran all over the place. In the background was the loud, annoying Mexican music with no rhythm, Ernestine decided, and how could anyone dance to it? They paid the bill, left a small tip, the food heavy in their stomachs, grabbed their bags and slowly walked back to the car three blocks away. He was concerned that it may not be there, heisted by some young criminals: it was sitting there amongst a few other vehicles with dirt and dents in them. They quickly got in, started the engine, and left south towards home.

# CHAPTER 11

On the trip back, around midafternoon, Ernestine began to doze off. Maybe the heavy food and excitement had got to her, John mused, as he tried to pass by the crush of traffic surrounding him, the stop and go, the humming of the cars attempting to move forward. He let her sleep as he entered the Irvine area, and the traffic was lighter. Ernestine stirred, breathed in, and woke up. She stared hazily at him.

"Wow, I was knocked out."

"You sure were, but it is okay. Must have been those beers."

"Must have," she replied, wiggling in her seat, and she stared at him intently. "Did you have a good time?"

"The best," he asserted. "We needed to get away from all the madness that has cropped up. LA is an exciting city; I would not mind living here if I had the right opportunity. We'll come again soon."

She shook her head in assent and put her delicate hand with the long fingernails on his arm, rubbing it in affection and possession. Suddenly, she probed, "Are you happy with me?"

He gave her a quick side glance, startled, confused. "Happy? Of course. You are my life. You know I love you, and don't forget it."

"Are you glad you met me?" she skillfully continued.

"What? Are you crazy? If it wasn't for you, where would I be? I'd be lost, you know that… You are just testing me."

Looking out the window, the wind flowing in with the cacophony of noise, she said, "A girl needs to hear it every so often. She needs to feel important and wanted. No regrets?"

He paused. "No, about marrying you? No regrets. I never look back. We are a team, solid, and will have a great life together."

There was a hiatus as she mused, then added, "It is sort of odd, hard to explain. I feel once I made the decision to drop Spencer and date outside of my race, I became free, no hang-ups, no rules to follow, no being in a square box. I was liberated and liked it. Do you feel the same way?"

"Of course," he emphasized with fervor. "I said this before, I came from a stodgy environment with parents, devout Catholics, telling us to do this, don't do that, feel guilty about everything; you could never be happy or perfect because everything was a sin. I was sick of it. I still believe in God, but he must be a benevolent God, not someone made up by the Church to be punitive and angry… Life was pitiful living at home with my mom and brother, so sterile. Yes, I feel free for the first time in my life, but more than that. I became a real person who accepts all people for who they are."

"You sound so philosophical," she replied with a frown. "But you have a point. It was odd that we met by chance in a theater when our lives were so divisive, life uncertain, you know—"

"I see it, honey, as destiny. It was meant to be. I believe that people that are different is a strength, and that is the glue that binds them together. If everyone married someone who is white, like themselves, there would be no excitement, no room for growth. How did we get on this topic?" he questioned, squinting.

"It's a good topic to me. It's important to know your partner, what makes him tick, what drives him, how he sees the future." She added, sipping water, "And I hope you will see a future with a few children. Right?"

"I like how you put things, and slide them right in. Just don't rush me, babe. Let's get married first. I am a little bit nervous about kids; just look at me and my family. I grew up with arguments, fights, no money, constant yelling, my dad using the strap on us when we got out of line. You know the drill; you went through that craziness and abuse, too."

"Let's not go there, too painful, sweetie. All we can do is to lead our own lives. We can't undo what our parents did or said; they must live with their mistakes. It was a different time that they lived in."

He blurted out, "It doesn't excuse their behavior, the ignorance, the ignoring of your kids. They could not keep the marriage together and who are the stupid ones? Them; it was all on them and their responsibility to be adults, and they failed at it. I think about it a lot, and the day my dad walked out on us. I was left with my mother and surly brother to deal with; it was like being in prison with a sentence, a punishment. Somehow, I graduated, found a job, and moved out. I do have nightmares about it, of being trapped in the house, unable to escape. Is that not weird?"

He stopped his tirade, his confession, depleted, angry, face puckered, frowning, uttering a few curse words under his breath. He began to sweat.

"I didn't mean to get you upset. But it is good to talk about stuff, issues."

"Sure, if you say so," he sardonically responded. "Dear old mom and dad, and that ass of a brother trying to ruin everyone's lives with his antics. It's a wonder I am still sane."

She commiserated with him. "If it's any consolation, my parents were no charmers themselves, either. I just don't talk about it much or reveal all the details. I remember Brenda used to sneak out at night through the bedroom screen to hook up with some dude. My mom would find out she was missing, and man... she got the wet strap across her fanny, and she would traipse into the house high. Mom was insulted and shocked by this. She must have been seventeen or so. But she kept doing it over and over, like a cat and mouse game; mom would be irate, yelling, hitting, giving out lectures, out of control. I guess some of her anger was because my dad was not there to deal with it. And you want to talk about my dad: he used to pull me by the hair for no reason, yelling, drunk, cursing, always arguing with mom over money. He was accused of being in the streets, spending our income, chasing all types of women who would have sex with him, white ones, too. Yeah, I know your pain."

"I hope they don't bring their attitudes and hang-ups to our wedding; that is my fear. When you get so many people together at one time, you will always have gossip, envy, distrust, and maybe a few choice words. Hell, maybe the ceremony will appease and erase any doubters or family issues."

"Just to let you know," she defended him, "we are certainly not going to put up with anyone who doesn't want to be there. We should be concentrating on being happy and embracing the majority of folks who support us, period. There will be no troublemakers there, none. My friends down the street, if they are invited, if they don't like you, they don't like me."

"Good. I am glad to hear that. I must still tell my father; he's cool, but his silly antics… I fear he might have an argument with my mom or brother, who hates him. Maybe we should not dwell on it so much, it makes us look insecure. We just came from a nice little trip and now we are reduced to the pisshole of life."

Lightly, she answered, "You never know how things will turn out. We are going to be too busy to notice any shenanigans by some stupid family members. I can see crazy Brenda igniting the crowd, dancing hard on the floor, and finding a man to latch on to." She giggled, shaking her head in fondness. "Yes, dear Brenda will spice everything up, and we have to monitor her alcohol intake. When she has too many, she can say the wildest things and pick a fight. I will have mom keep an eye on her, she's good at that. It's going to be a celebration and comedy show at the same time. You laugh at it."

The car droned on past a traffic light as they entered the environs of San Diego in the fading sunlight near Oceanside, rambling endlessly ahead, past canyons, trees, brush, hills, the nuclear power plant, a few cars on the side of the road for some reason, cruising past the checkpoint, state rest areas where vans and cars were parked, watching the sunset and water.

With the air flowing through the window, Ernestine drifted back in her past to Spencer Haygood, her old boyfriend. His presence kept reemerging as they talked of the wedding. She recalled an argument in his apartment over four years ago; vivid, destructive, and alarming. She could not find Spencer for three days; no phone calls, no contact. Heavy-set Spencer, all six foot three of him, disappeared off the face of the earth. She initially wondered if something had happened to him, if he was hurt, or in a hospital. On that fourth day, Ernestine showed up at his old apartment, knocked, and he answered the door with a surly, disturbed demeanor. He had been drinking and several beer bottles were on the coffee table, with food wrappers strewn everywhere, as if he was angry or in turmoil. He told her he had been visiting a relative out of town, and he slurred his words as he spoke. He was not convincing, was evasive of who the person was and what he had been doing. Ernestine remembered that she stood there, in his living room, arms folded, and eyed him in distrust. She smelled a faint scent of perfume and accused him of cheating; she went toward his bedroom, and instinctively opened his dresser drawer, found a pair of unknown panties there, came back with them and threw them in his face. She said, right then and there, with finality, that it was over, and she left him there in his misery with a sour face.

Her life now was so different: no person hiding in shadows, no fake, evasive answers, no bold stares, no man chasing the skirt of another woman. John, she knew, was the antithesis of Spencer; he was loyal, dedicated, not complicated, and you could trust him with your life. Why did this Spencer want to get back together? Why did he go back to her mother's house? It was all useless, insane jealousy, a dumb homeboy struggling to find an existence, a man who was a cheater, cheating life, hurting everyone around him, unaware of his stupidity; and the telltale sign of this, that she did not realize until late in that relationship, is that he had few close friends, and the ones he had seemed too distant from him or were short-lived. It was something about his character, his persona, that disgusted people. She saw this as sad. As the car drove south, she was thankful that she did not get pregnant by Spencer or marry him in desperation. She fervently hoped that Spencer would not just show up at the wedding, getting the date and address from her mother. She quickly dispelled this idea because he would be too embarrassed to be there, as a second-rate loser, and all eyes would be on him in derision. No, Spencer Haygood would not show up for the wedding because he was already dating another girl and screwing her.

"Tomorrow is your birthday, the big two-four. What would you like to do?" Ernestine pleasantly asked.

"You decide."

"Well, for starters, I'll bring over a big cake with twenty-four candles. And then, we will go out and have a nice steak dinner, my treat. Or better yet, if you come over to my crib, we can have more privacy, if you know what I mean." She said this with her eyebrows raised and one finger on her half-opened lips.

"I get what you mean, cool girl... Your place tomorrow around three," he said with no emphasis, stolid, leering at her, her trim figure in the tight jeans, excited, her appearance still fresh, even though they had been gone the whole day in the heat and smog. *How does she always maintain her makeup?* he asked himself. *Always presentable, always lively, always radiant.* Most of the girls he knew, and had seen on the street, looked tired, and did not care about appearances, and took life as it was.

"If you play your cards right, buster, you'll have a birthday you will never forget," she added.

He said nothing. He just nodded and pulled into the parking lot and parked. They sat in the car a few moments to collect themselves, tired of the grueling drive. They smiled at each other, exited the vehicle, and grabbed their bags from the trunk. On the way, John went to the mailbox to retrieve his mail. John put several letters in his left hand, and they climbed the steep steps to the corner apartment and entered. The air was stale inside, and it was silent and still. Moving forward, music could be faintly heard from Ron's room. The sun was still out in the fading heat emanating the living room as John opened the blinds and window. The bags were dropped on the floor by the couch as they listened to the rock music and stared at each other.

"You don't think your roommate will mind me being here?" Ernestine nervously asked.

"Mind?" he said with a smirk, pushing his hand to the side. "It is none of his business. He needs to stay busy and find a girlfriend," he added, annoyed, sorting out his mail.

"It seem a lot of times I feel like I am imposing on his space, and I don't like that... Another reason for you to move in with me. It's time," she asserted as she moved away to the couch and flipped on the television, idly changing channels. She appeared unhappy or exhausted from the drive.

John picked out a small white envelope from the stack and turned it over; it was addressed to him, with no return address. "This is odd; wonder what this is. Probably junk mail." He opened the letter, and inside it was the snapshot photo of Anna, Susan, and himself smiling under the tree at campus, the photo taken in 1979, his second year of college. In the envelope was a small note, undated, which ran thus:

John,

If you get this letter, you know what happened. I am passing this on to you so you can remember us, the Three Musketeers, from our college days. I find life very hard and do not want to continue. Take care.

Always, Susan

John shuddered as he stared at the note and photo. It was so unreal to him that Susan no longer existed, almost impossible that someone so young and educated would throw her life away. He began to cry, wiped a tear from his cheek, standing directly in the middle of the living room, breathing forcibly, and gazed at Ernestine. She looked up from the television, perturbed, rose and querulously asked, "What is the matter? Bad news?"

"Yes, read this," he quietly said. He passed the envelope over to her and she read it listlessly, frowning.

Then her face uplifted. "What does it mean?"

"Nothing," he calmly said, taking the photo and note from her. "Really nothing. It's over and I don't want to talk or remember this any more." He walked to the kitchen trash can and dropped the photo and note in it.

Ernestine was staring at him, confused, not sure what to say about the cryptic letter. All she knew was that there was pain in the room, her fiancé's whole demeanor had changed from the trip to one of confusion and despair.

A moment elapsed, and he said, "I'm sorry I got you mixed up in all of this. I did not expect to come home from a nice outing and have this. It is as if she is haunting us, and I will not let that happen. God, she was so stupid, and for what? For a thrill. Now she's dead, and we can do nothing about it." He searched her face for help and validation.

"Life goes on," she maturely commented. "I know a few friends that killed themselves by drug overdoses, gone way too early. Life is not easy at times."

"You know, Ernestine, I'm faithful always to you… and love you deeply," he replied emotionally, sniffing. His voice trembled. "Don't ever forget that."

"I know, I know; you don't have to prove anything to me, ever. You already did by giving me your love, your life, sharing all you have with me. That photo and note is nothing, just a sickness talking."

He paused. "I guess you are right. I was afraid you would leave me because of all of it."

Quietly, she answered, "Never, not until the end of time."

He moved towards her, grabbed her tightly around the waist, his eyes searching, directed at hers. "Life is for the living; no guilt, no shame, right?" He pointed out the living room window and continued, "Life, it's out there."

"Your life is with me, no matter where it leads us, babe," Ernestine answered as they continued to hug each other in silence.